Aftermath

MANCINI LEGACY SERIES
BOOK 1

NATALIE ARTHUR

The Mancini Legacy Series books are all stand alone with NO cheating and HEA.

Even though they are standalone, they are best enjoyed if read in order. There is also mention of characters from my Cimaruta MC Chicago Series.

 Created with Vellum

Acknowledgments

Jessica, you are summer and I am winter. Always.

Danni, this journey is so crazy! Thank you for being here with me!

JD, thank you for spending late nights with and making sure I listened even when I didn't want to. Love you.

Nicole, I'm forever grateful that you're in my life.

Carissa, thank you for everything you do.

Arthur, you've always supported me no matter how crazy my ideas are. I love you so much.

Mom, you've always been my biggest supporter and I don't know where I'd be without you.

Caoimhe-Lea, you drive me absolutely fucking crazy. I wouldn't have it any other way. Love you.

Taye, and everyone I'm forgetting who has supported

my crazy ideas and continue to be with me, thank you. I truly couldn't do this without all of you.

Information

No part of this book or graphics were made with AI.
HUMAN CREATION ONLY

Aftermath has NO cheating with a guaranteed HEA.
It is the first book in my Mancini Legacy Series.

There are not a lot of dark moments or dark issues in
my books, there still are the occasions that have to do
with kidnapping, domestic abuse, and assault.

Check out my website for current news and trigger
warnings.
Mancini Legacy and Cimaruta MC family trees.
Nataliearthurbooks.com

Mancini Legacy and Cimaruta MC Dictionary

Cage - Motorized vehicle with four wheels. (Cars)

Chicago Panthers - Professional baseball team.

Chicago Redhawks - Professional hockey team.

Cimaruta MC, Chicago - Chicago Motorcycle club, Mother charter

Cut - Vest that patched in members of the MC wear to identify who they are and their rank.

Lake Renegade Township - Town owned by the Mancini family.

Lucciola Island - 'Firefly' Island, owned by the Mancini family and located in Massachusetts.

Lucciola Memorial Hospital - Hospital in Lake Renegade Township.

Mancini Grill - 5-star restaurant located inside the Legacy Hotel.

Rockers - Top rocker has the club's name on it, the bottom rocker has the club's location.

Sprite Lake Village - Town in Illinois, owned by the Laurent family.

The Legacy Hotel - Hotel in downtown Chicago owned by the Mancini family.

Galway - Town in Ireland.

ITALIAN

Amore - Love.

Coglione - Asshole.

Colomba mia - My dove.

Cugino - Cousin.

Cuore mio - My heart.

Dolcezza - Sweetness.

Famiglia - Family.

Figlio - Son.

Fratello - Brother.

Il mio mondo - My world.

Il mio pinguino - My penguin.

Mai Andato - Never Gone.

Mi dispiace - I'm sorry.

Mi passerotta - My little sparrow.

Nonno - Grandfather.

Nonna - Grandmother.

Ti abbiamo aspettato - We waited for you.

Ti voglio bene - I love you.

Zio - Uncle.

Zia - Aunt.

IRISH

Aintín - Aunty

Is í Gàidhlig ár gcéad teanga - Gaelic is our first language.

M'anam - My soul

Mo stór - My treasure.

FRENCH

D'accord petite sœur - Okay little sister

Je t'aime et Lorenzo - I love you and Lorenzo

Je t'aime - I love you

Je vous aime tous les deux - I love you both

Princesse - Princess

Toujours - Always

Toujours mes frères - Always my brothers

Tu es ma princesse - You are my princess

MANCINI FAMILY

Pietro & Alessia
Grandparents

Enea (T)
Son

Antonio (T)
Son

Leonardo (T)
Son

Gráinne
Daughter-in-law

Rosaura
Daughter-in-law

Sebastiano*
Grandson

Salvatore^
Grandson

Domenico*
Grandson

Fiorella^
Granddaughter

Lorenzo+
Grandson

Gianluca^
Grandson

Giovanna+
Granddaughter

Rowan
Great Grandson

(T) = Triplets
* = Twins
+ = Twins
^ = Triplets

MANCINI FAMILY

Antonio (T)

Enea (T)

Gráinne

Leonardo (T)

Rosaura

Sebastiano*

Salvatore^

Schuyler

Sansone

Fiorella^

Domenico*

Lorenzo+

Gianluca^

Giovanna+

Declan

Rowan

(T) = Triplets
* = Twins
+ = Twins
^ = Triplets

LIAM & RIOGHNACH
GRANDPARENTS

AIDEN
SON

GRÁINNE
DAUGHTER

ÉLODIE
DAUGHTER=IN LAW

ENEA
SON-IN-LAW

EMMERSON

ELIAS

EASTON *

EZRA *

EDEN

GRANDKIDS

SEBASTIANO *

DOMENICO *

LORENZO *

GIOVANNA *

GRANDKIDS

TWINS *

Laurent Family

Contents

Prequel

Mancini Legacy
Prudential
MANCINI LEGACY SERIES BOOK PREQUEL
NATALIE ARTHUR

Chapter One

Twenty-Three Years Ago...
They took our two-year-old twins and our
family has never been the same.

Enea

The war between the Mancinis and Laurents started long ago, before our families ever came to America.

It was a constant battle for territory. At some point, it became personal for the Mancinis and the Laurents, who were fighting for control over parts of Central Europe. Neither family gained the upper hand, and for a while, it seemed to have calmed down. That's when my papà decided it was time to move our family to

Chicago, Illinois, to expand our business. My brothers and I were three.

Years later, we found out that the Laurents had moved to Illinois as well. They settled in Springfield, which is a few hours away from Lake Renegade Township. We aren't sure if they chose to move there because of us or if it was a coincidence.

When it was time for me to take over the family business from my papà, the animosity between us and the Laurents started to grow again. Dorian Laurent was taking over for his father, and territory was the goal once more. We were fighting each other for the same routes to run our guns and drugs out of Illinois.

During this time, my youngest twins, who were two years old, were kidnapped and murdered. The people who took them sent pictures as proof of the kills, and also as a threat to the rest of our family to show what they were capable of. If they could kill children, what wouldn't they do? Because of that, we were all forced to take extra precautions. I couldn't take the chance that anyone else would get hurt.

I suspected the Laurents were the ones who took our children, but without proof, I couldn't retaliate. If they weren't to blame, that would just make things worse. Even after seeing the pictures, my family never gave up hope that our babies could still be alive.

Giovanna

When my alarm screeches at me, I stretch and yawn. I can hear my brothers making noise outside, so I get up and go over to the window. I look down on them, watching as they spar together. Their weapon of choice for today? Swords—and I see blood. I shake my head, knock on the window, point, and laugh. They all look up at me and wave. Goofballs.

My papa is Dorian Laurent and he's the head of the Springfield mafia here in Illinois. We lost our mamma in a car accident when I was six.

It's winter break and I have some time off from school. No matter what's going on in our lives, we always spend the holidays at home as a family. After the new year, my twin brother Lorenzo and I will head back to Crimson University in Cambridge, Massachusetts.

I just started med school and Lorenzo is studying to be a lawyer. We own a house in Cambridge so that Lorenzo and I don't have to live in the dorms. This also makes it easier for our brothers and dad to come visit us whenever they want.

The home where we grew up is in Sprite Lake Village. It's about three hours southwest of downtown Chicago. The whole village is ours.

There's another clan that lives about three and a half hours northeast of us in Lake Renegade Township. They're the Mancini family, the Chicago mafia. From what my papa has told us, there's been bad blood between us for as long as anyone can remember. It started back in Europe and followed us here to the

United States. For the last twenty years, there's been a tentative truce between our families. But my papa has always forbidden us from going anywhere near their town and still does to this day.

After showering, I head downstairs to have breakfast. Jacques, my bodyguard, is sitting with my dad. They eat breakfast together every morning. Jacques has been my guard since the day I turned sixteen. Before that, he was an enforcer for my dad, so I've known him for most of my life.

"Hi, Papa." I kiss his cheek as I grab some breakfast. "Morning, Jacques."

Jacques gives me a grunt and shoves more food into his mouth. I snort while I shake my head at him.

"*Princesse.*" Papa smiles as he turns to hug me. "Have I said how much I love it when you're all home with me?" He chuckles,

"You say that every time," I tease him.

"Well, it's the truth. The house always seems so quiet without everyone here."

"That's because you have five sons and they're really, really noisy." I chuckle. "Did you know they're playing with swords right now?"

"Yeah, I saw them taking the swords outside. I figured as long as I don't hear any crying, they're okay." He smirks.

I giggle. "There was some blood, but not enough to make them stop."

"Boys." He shakes his head.

Giovanna

Being back at school is always nice—it means I'm that much closer to becoming a doctor—something I've wanted since I lost my mother.

This is our last weekend before classes start back up, and I want to get out of the house.

I grab my jacket and purse, making sure I have my phone and keys. "I'm leaving!" I call out to my brothers.

Christophe and Lorenzo come walking into the foyer. "Wait! I'm going too!" They both say.

Our papa and Christophe came back with us after the holidays. They're staying for a few weeks. Our other brothers, identical twins Fabien and François, are supposed to be coming up next week. Only Jérôme wasn't able to take time off, he's doing his ER rotation right now and the holidays are always super busy.

I sigh as I see my oldest brother and my youngest. They look so different, Christophe with his bright blue eyes and light brown hair; Lorenzo with his crystal clear blue-green eyes and auburn hair. I watch them run towards the car and I get into the passenger seat as fast as I can because I know something is going to happen. Jacques is beside me, laughing as we both watch the scene unfold.

Christophe trips Lorenzo so that he can get to the car first. I think he's forgotten that Jacques beat them both to the car and is already warming it up.

I snicker at them. "You know I can shop alone, right?" I stick my tongue out at Chris. Lorenzo gets up and flips Chris off.

"What's the fun in that?" He laughs, pushing me into the back seat. He tells Jacques to get in the passenger seat so he can drive. Jacques grumbles, but he gets out and walks around the car, since he's too big to just climb over the console. Lorenzo hops in the back with me. It's such an ordeal just to go to the mall.

"Cambridge Mall?" he asks.

"Yeah, I don't feel like going far. I just wanted to get out of the house for a bit."

Chris pulls into the covered parking lot, then we all get out and walk into the mall. As I look around, I see two identical guys staring at me. They look like Domenico Mancini, goalie for my favorite hockey team, the Chicago Redhawks. I frown as I look back at them; they feel strangely familiar. Not because they look like Domenico—it's like I should know them, but I don't. I brush the feeling off and keep walking.

Sebastiano

"Do you see them?" I ask my identical twin brother, Domenico. He nods without taking his eyes off them.

"She looks like Mamma. But there's no way, right?" he whispers. He's taking his phone out of his pocket. I watch him covertly snap some pictures of her to send to our Papà.

"That one guy she's with looks like us, Dom. But that's impossible! Did you send the pics to Papà?"

"Sent now." He continues to stare at them. Dom's phone buzzes.

Enea: WHO IS THAT?

Domenico: Don't know, we just saw her here in Cambridge. There's a guy with her who looks like me and Bastian

Enea: Follow them. Find out who they are. I'm on my way. We'll be there in less than an hour. Keep me posted

Domenico: Sì, Papà. Safe travels, see you soon

"Could they really be Enzo and Gia?" Dom asks me as we continue to follow them.

"I don't know," I say as my voice shakes.

Our younger twin siblings were kidnapped and murdered when they were two years old. Our parents were sent proof of their deaths—pictures of the babies wrapped up in their blankets, covered in blood. But looking at those two, I swear it's them. That girl, she looks like my mamma, and the guy? He looks like us, like our papà. I feel a strange pull to them that I have only ever felt with my twin and my family. But it can't be...

There's two other guys with them. One looks like he's following them, like a bodyguard. The women in our family have bodyguards too. But the other's way too casual around them, maybe a family member? Close friend?

Giovanna

After about an hour of walking around, I'm still trying to ignore the two guys following us.

"Are you okay?" I hear Lorenzo whisper to me.

"There's two guys following us. I don't think they're dangerous, I actually feel like we should know them somehow," I whisper to him. He looks at the twins and nods. "They look like our Hawks goalie." I keep an eye on them while we walk.

"I thought it was just me," he whispers back. I shake my head at him.

Jacques stays close to me—I know he notices the twins too.

"I'm going to the restroom," Chris says to us.

We nod at Chris, still distracted by the twins.

"Are you okay?"

"Huh? Oh sorry. I thought I saw Domenico Mancini. You know, goalie for my Hawks." I smile.

Chris laughs. "Only you would think you're seeing him here in Cambridge. Meet you at the food court?"

"Sounds good. I was just going to say I'm hungry." He chuckles as he kisses my head and goes to find a restroom. After he leaves, I turn and stalk over to where the twins are with Lorenzo and Jacques trailing behind me.

"Giovanna—" Jacques tries to warn me, but I ignore him and keep walking.

"Who are you and why are you following us?" I ask sharply, glaring at the two of them. They have the same crazy blue-green eyes that Lorenzo has.

"I-I'm sorry. We didn't mean to scare you," one of them says.

"You remind us of someone," says the other.

"I'm Sebastiano and this is Domenico," Sebastiano says.

"Holy shit, it is you! Domenico Mancini, goalie for the Chicago Redhawks," I say as I stare at Domenico. I see him slowly nod yes. "But why would you be following us?"

As we're talking, I see four enormous men walking towards us. The one leading the group looks a lot like Enea Mancini, head of the Chicago mafia. The very person my papa told us to stay away from. He comes over and stands in front of me, his eyes filling with tears. It's at this point that I realize Lorenzo looks similar to him and the twins. Jacques is trying to get to me but the other three guys are blocking him.

"Who are you?" I ask as I stare at him, needing confirmation.

"My name is Enea Mancini," he says softly. "What's your name?"

"Uh. Gi-Giovanna. You—you're the head of the Chicago mafia," I say. Lorenzo comes to stand beside me and takes my hand.

"And you?" he asks Lorenzo.

Chapter Three

Lorenzo

"I'm Lorenzo." I look at all of them and pull Giovanna to my side, holding her tight. I can feel her shaking.

"*Mamma mia*," one of the twins says softly. I honestly can't tell them apart. They really are identical.

Enea pulls Giovanna away from me and wraps his giant arms around her. I try to stop him just as she tries to step away from him.

"We thought you were both dead," he chokes out.

I continue to try and pull my sister away from Enea, but he only holds on tighter. There's a part of me that wants him to let her go, yet another part feels a strange comfort in watching him hold her. Before I can react, he pulls me into the hug with her. There's no escaping him.

"Arturo, Marco, close the store. Tell the employees they will get the full day's pay, but it's time to go home," he says to two of the big guys with him. "Grady, you keep an eye on him." The third one—who I'm guessing is Grady—has a firm grip on Jacques, which is a hard thing to do. Jacques is a big guy, but this guy is even bigger than him. The two who Enea called Arturo and Marco turn and walk away as Enea continues to hold us. I don't know why we're following him, but something in me wants to know why he's acting like he knows us.

Enea leads us to a storefront with the third guy following behind, still keeping Jacques in check. I'm trying to get my thoughts in order while listening to him talk, but I can't wrap my head around what he's saying. I don't understand why he's crying. I keep a close eye on my sister and hold on to her hand, following Enea to the storefront.

"What are you talking about? Where are you taking us?" I ask him.

He turns to look at me, "You're my children. I'm taking you to the shop we own so that we can talk. Please don't cry, Giovanna." He looks at her with tears in his own eyes. "I would never hurt you."

"You're crazy! You need to let my sister go." I'm about to lose my cool and try to break away. But one of the guys nudges me forward.

Finally Enea stops. "Look at me, *figlio*. Tell me you don't see yourself in me, in Sebastiano and Domenico."

He motions for the twins to come closer. "You have your mother's eyes, just like them. My beautiful Giovanna, you are everything I thought you would look like as an adult. You have my eyes, but you look like your mother, down to your beautiful curly hair. All of you have your mam's auburn hair."

Giovanna and I stare at the three of them. This has to be a dream. Real life doesn't happen like this.

"We need to call our papa," I say, my voice shaking.

Enea frowns.

"Who's your papà?" we hear another voice ask.

"Our papa is Dorian Laurent," Giovanna says as they close in tighter around us.

"Please, you have to listen to me," Enea says as he watches us. "You're my children. My youngest twins. I know it. I feel it in my soul. For some reason, they kept your first names. You're Lorenzo Aonghus Mancini and you, my baby, are Giovanna Aoife Mancini." He chokes up. "Has Dorian told you about the war between our families? Our twins went missing twenty-three years ago. We were never sure who took them, although we suspected it was the Laurents. Now, I know for sure that Dorian Laurent stole you from us. We were told you were dead. But you're not. You're here. Alive." He starts leading us to the store again.

I don't get the feeling he's lying to us. I try to remember what our papa has said to us about the Mancinis throughout our lives. The only thing that stands out is him saying that we were to avoid them at all costs. That our lives would be in danger because of the war. What if the real danger our papa was worried about was Giovanna and me being recognized by the Mancinis?

We see Chris coming towards us, and he looks furious.

"Get your hands off my brother and sister!" he yells as he tries to get closer. But he's stopped by the massive man that stayed behind.

"Back off," he warns Chris.

We hear Jacques explaining to Chris what Enea just told us.

"What the fuck? Fine! You can deal with our papa," Chris spits out, pulling his phone out to call our papa.

I hear Enea laughing as we get to the store. It's called Amore, Italian for love. It looks like they rent or sell wedding dresses and tuxedos.

"Si. Call your papa, tell him Enea Mancini knows what he did with my twins. And that I'll be taking them home with me," he says to Chris.

"What are you talking about? They're my brother and sister!" Chris exclaims. He's looking at Enea like he's insane. "This is proof that you Mancinis are fucking crazy! Our papa is on his way."

Enea herds us through the door.

I look at Enea. "Why are you saying these things about our papa?" I ask him the second we're all inside. "My papa is the kindest man I know. He would never do what you're saying he did." I can see the hurt in Enea's eyes as he listens to me.

"Tell me something. Do you look like him? Or any of his sons?" he asks Giovanna and me.

I think about it and slowly shake my head no. "But so what?"

I've always secretly wondered why Giovanna and I don't look like my papa or my mamma. My older brothers look like Dorian, but we don't. Dorian is French, with blond hair and blue eyes. Nadia was Italian, well actually Sicilian, so she had dark hair and eyes. Giovanna and I are fair-skinned and have curly auburn hair.

"You're my children," he says again. He pulls a picture out of his wallet and shows it to us. "This is your mother, Gráinne. She never gave up hope that you could be alive." His eyes fill with tears.

My heart quickens, and I freeze. There's a striking resemblance between Giovanna and the woman in the picture. My eyes are exactly the same as hers, as Sebastiano and Domenico's. I look at Giovanna; she looks stunned, staring at the picture of Gráinne. Then she looks into Enea's eyes, which are the same starburst pattern of green that she always said didn't match the Laurent name.

Giovanna

I see something in Enea's eyes. I start to feel a tightening in my stomach, and I know he isn't lying.

I look over at Lorenzo. "You remember something, don't you?"

"I remember being called Enzo," he says slowly.

That's a weird memory because we've never called him anything but Lorenzo.

"We called you Enzo. I couldn't say Lorenzo when I was little. No matter how much I tried, all I could say was Enzo," Sebastiano says. His voice breaks, and he steps closer to Lorenzo to hug him.

"We called you Gia. I tried to call you Giovanna, but I couldn't," Dom says softly, grabbing me and holding me tight.

I look at Lorenzo as my eyes get bigger. I've never been called anything but Giovanna. Never Gia. But hearing him say it triggers something in me, a long-forgotten memory of hearing a child's voice calling me that.

My tears fall freely as I let Domenico hug me. We hear a commotion outside and I look up to see my papa, Dorian. We can hear him yelling at the men that Enea called Grady and Marco. They're holding him back, preventing him from coming into the store.

"GET AWAY FROM MY CHILDREN, MANCINI!" Dorian yells from outside. There's a few curious shoppers who are looking over to see what all the commotion is about.

I stare at the man I have known my whole life as my papa.

Enea looks out the door and sees people slowing down to stare into the shop as they walk by. He motions for Arturo to let Dorian and Christophe in. After they step inside, he locks the door behind them, then draws the shades.

"Tell me he is lying, Papa..." I start to sob and run over to him, trying to keep from exploding. "Say you didn't take Lorenzo and me from them all those years ago." My tears flow as I raise my voice.

"Princesse. Please, you know me. I would never hurt you or your brothers," he says, pulling me into a hug.

I can see Enea holding back his rage when Dorian calls me his princess and pulls me into his arms.

"You're not answering my questions, Papa," I say, pushing away from him so that I can look him in the eye. "Did you or did you not do what Enea is saying?" I'm so angry, it feels like my whole body is on fire. I don't understand why he isn't answering my questions.

"Tu es ma princesse..." You are my princess. "You have to understand, we were at war. They left you all alone. I heard crying and found both of you huddled in a corner—I took both of you to keep you safe," he tries to explain.

"Papa...you...you kidnapped them?" Chris says in disbelief. He immediately stops fighting Grady. "How could you do that? They were babies!"

I watch Dorian drop to his knees and put his head in his hands. My own head swivels as I look to Enea, then Dorian, then back to Enea.

I'm trying to wrap my head around everything that I've just learned. My papa isn't my papa. My real father is the man that I was taught to fear my whole life. Yet looking at Enea, I feel no fear. I feel comfort in being close to him. I finally go over to him. "I'm sorry that I don't remember you," I say as I wipe my tears and let him hug me again.

"Please, you're my children. *Je t'aime et Lorenzo.* Please," Dorian begs as he watches Enea hold me. *I love you and Lorenzo.*

I don't doubt that Dorian loves us. He has never shown us anything but love. But he's not our papa. He's the man who kidnapped us, took us from our real family. Dorian admitted that he sent pictures to the Mancini family. Pictures that looked like bloodied babies wrapped up in blankets. He says the were fake, but who does that? What kind of monster steals babies, then tells their family they're dead? My whole body feels numb. I don't know whether to scream or cry right now.

"You're my babies. I thought you were gone and it killed me every day. Your mamma...oh god, your mamma won't believe we found you both. My children." He keeps saying we're his children, like if he stops saying it, we'll disappear. "I'll never let anything happen to you again. I promise." I finally hug him back and my tears soak his shirt. I can feel his chest heaving.

I look over at Bastian and Dom. They come and wrap their arms tightly around us.

I see Enea's guys grabbing Dorian. No matter what we've learned today, I can't let them hurt him.

"Please. Just let him go. He never hurt us. You can't hurt him," I beg Enea. I go over to Dorian and hug him. "*Je t'aime*, Papa. But I don't know if I'll ever understand how you could do this. I don't know if I can forgive you, I don't know anything anymore. I feel like our whole life was a lie." I take a deep breath and step back to look at him.

"I couldn't kill you or Lorenzo. When I took you home, your mamma was so happy to have a daughter. After we lost her, I had to keep you safe. I promised," Dorian says, trying to grab onto Lorenzo and me again.

I step back out of reach. If Dorian hadn't admitted to taking us, I would never even consider leaving with Enea. But he did. He stole us from our real family and I can't just go back to my old life like nothing's changed.

I turn to Chris. "Please take Papa home. Make sure he's okay." I hug him tightly and hold back the tears that are threatening to fall again. "You'll always be my brother. I promise you that," I whisper.

"I didn't know, Giovanna." His tears are falling. "Please don't shut me out. I understand you're angry at Papa, but please don't shut the rest of us out."

Lorenzo

"We won't. We just need time," I say to Chris.

I see the tears in his eyes, and I know he understands. They'll always be our brothers, but what Dorian did is unforgivable. I'm barely keeping it together. I need to be strong for Giovanna, so I'll deal with my feelings later.

"*Je vous aime tous les deux,*" Chris says. *I love you both.*

Jacques comes over to give Giovanna and me a hug. I know she's going to miss him. He's been with her for the last six years. I can see the pain in her eyes as she says goodbye.

"If you need me, call me and I'll come," he says to her.

"Thank you. Take care of all of them. Promise me," she answers.

"I promise." He joins Christophe and Dorian.

"*Je t'aime aussi,* Chris." We watch him walk away with Dorian and Jacques. He keeps turning to look at us.

I wipe my face and hold on to Giovanna while she sobs. I turn to look at Enea.

"You promise to leave them alone?" I stare at him. He frowns and sighs. After what feels like hours, he nods.

"If that's what you're asking me to do, sì. I'll do that for the both of you."

"Thank you." My heart is breaking as I watch them walk away.

Giovanna

I don't know what to say so I stay quiet. We follow the group to the car. We get in with Enea, Grady and Sebastiano. Domenico, Marco and the other guard, Arturo, get into a second car to follow us. I'm really nervous because we're about to meet our real mother. After Nadia died, it was hard being the only girl surrounded by boys. I know Dorian dated, but he never brought anyone home.

As we're driving, I notice we're heading to the marina.

"Do you live on a boat?"

Enea chuckles. "No, amore, we live on one of the islands. We named it Lucciola Island."

"Firefly Island." I smile. "I love fireflies."

Lorenzo and I follow them to a sleek powerboat. The name on it is Mai Andato which means "Never Gone." We board it, cast off, and head to their island.

"This boat was named for you and Lorenzo. We never once forgot about either of you," Enea explains.

I'm mesmerized watching him talk. Lorenzo looks so much like him and the twins. But Enea's eyes—it's like staring into my own in a mirror. I've always thought my eyes were such an odd green color, they're actually a cluster of different shades of green. Now I know where they came from.

"Your home is impressive," I say as we dock. And it

is—it's a Cape Cod-style house with a deck wrapping all the way around it.

"Thank you, amore." Enea smiles. "This is one of our vacation homes."

I reach for Lorenzo's hand. "I'm scared, Lorenzo," I whisper.

"I got you, Giovanna. There's nothing we can't do together. This is our family." Hearing him say that makes me stand up straighter. He's right, we've always had each other and this is no different.

I see Gráinne come out the front door. I can't help but smile at her. She's even more stunning in person. She stops, visibly overwhelmed as she stares at Lorenzo and me, covering her mouth with her hands. I can see her openly weeping. She runs over and embraces me, then pulls Lorenzo in too.

"I never gave up hope you were alive." She has an Irish accent. It's lovely.

My tears flow as I hold my mother—my real mother. I'm unable to let go of her. She leads us into the house.

"We have so much to learn about each other. You're both so beautiful. Our babies are all back together!"

Enea smiles and kisses her.

Today has been a rollercoaster of emotions. I feel like I'm in a dream that I'll eventually wake up from. In one day, I've discovered my entire life was a lie. That my family isn't my family. And the people that are my family are the ones that I was told to stay away from my whole life. Oh, and my brother is the goalie for my favorite hockey team. This can't be real.

Aftermath

Mancini Legacy
AFTERMATH
MANCINI LEGACY SERIES BOOK ONE
NATALIE ARTHUR

Chapter One

Giovanna

We spent a week on Lucciola Island before coming back to Chicago. Lake Renegade Township reminds me a lot of Sprite Lake Village because both towns are centered around a beautiful lake with a nature preserve. There's a fence surrounding the entire thousand-acre property with a second fence built around the parcel of land that the family actually lives on. There are "No Trespassing" signs posted all along the inner fence and cameras that alert the main house if anyone gets near it. On the preserve side, there are twelve cabins, a designated area for tents, and full hookups for RVs. There are also bathrooms and showers.

I've started to explore the preserve and found a few small ponds to swim in. Then there's Lake Renegade. My nonno named it when he bought this property.

It takes about twenty minutes to drive from one end of town to the other. There's a motel and from what I've heard, it's always booked up. People really love our little town.

I do miss Sprite Lake sometimes, but I know I can never go back there.

Since we've been living in Lake Renegade Township, Enzo and I have been remembering little things from when we were younger. Of course, our parents have stories and pictures to fill in the first two years of our life. I still talk to my Laurent brothers weekly, but I haven't spoken to Dorian since that day at the mall. He was always good to us, but I don't know how to get past what happened yet.

I did question the lack of baby pictures for Lorenzo and me when we were with Dorian. He told us that they were lost in a fire and there were only a few pictures left of my Laurent brothers from when we were babies. Even though I thought it was odd, I never questioned it.

We've learned a lot about our family. Enea and his brothers came here from Italy when they were children. They're triplets—my father is the middle child, between my uncles Leonardo and Antonio. My Uncle Leo has three children with his wife, Rosaura.

They're triplets too—Salvatore, Fiorella, and Gianluca. Fiorella and I hit it off immediately. She's so full of life and being around her makes me feel like I have a sister —something I've always wanted. My Uncle Tonio is single and claims he'll never get married or have babies. My mother is from Galway, Ireland and has one older brother, Uncle Aiden.

When I was a Laurent, I had Jacques as my bodyguard. Now that we're back with our family, I have Grady. I haven't gotten to know him very well yet, but from what I can tell, he's a nice guy.

Tonight I'm going to my first live hockey game. I'm really excited to see Dom play. Dorian made sure we never went to a game—there was always some excuse as to why we couldn't go. But I did watch it on TV.

I remember when Dom was drafted by the Chicago Redhawks three years ago. He was one of three drafted that year along with Declan O'Reilly, defenseman, and Cillian McGregor, right wing. Cillian has been in a relationship with my cousin Fiorella for almost two years now.

I'm wearing Dom's jersey, number 99. It's the jersey he wore when he had his very first shutout game during his rookie year. He gave it to me the first night I spent back in our home in Lake Renegade. I chuckle hearing Dom yelling for everyone to hurry up. But we're waiting for our cousins to arrive and they're a little late. When they finally show up, Dom shoves them in the car before we can even say hello.

My brother arranged it so that we can tour the Redhawks locker room and meet the team. Meeting Declan O'Reilly in person? I might throw up. My plan is to hide behind one of my brothers or Papà. They're big enough to hide me. Yeah, that's a good plan. Hide. Then get to my seat and stay there.

As we're walking into the locker room, we hear someone yell, "***Call 911***!"

I shove my way through my brothers and see a man on the ground. I run over and gently push aside the guy that is kneeling near him so I can assess the man in distress. He isn't breathing and I don't feel a pulse, so I begin CPR right away.

"Assistant Coach Louis, he just grabbed his chest and collapsed," the guy (who I later realize is one of Dom's teammates) says to me.

"What's your name?" I ask while I start doing CPR on him.

"Milo," he says as he watches me work.

"Okay Milo, can you go get the AED?"

He looks at me with a puzzled expression.

"The automated external defibrillator," I explain. "There has to be one in the building."

"I'm on it." He gets up and runs off as the others are watching.

"Has someone called 911?" I ask.

"They're coming, Gia," I hear Dom say as I give him a slight nod and see Milo running back with the AED. I hook the coach up to it, then tell everyone to step back. I wait for it to analyze his heart.

"Shock indicated. Stand clear!" I call out. I make sure everyone is standing back, then press the button to shock the coach. I breathe a sigh of relief when I feel a faint pulse.

I hear the paramedics coming into the room.

"Male, possible cardiac arrest, CPR and one shock. Got a pulse, but still unresponsive," I say to them as they take over.

"Are you a doctor?" I hear one of them ask.

"Med student," I say.

"Good job, future doc, we got him from here." He winks at me as he helps his partner get Coach onto the gurney.

I watch them wheel the gurney out of the room. I feel someone put their arm around my shoulders and I look up at Dom.

"Good job, baby sis." I can see the pride in his face and that makes me grin even more.

The other players come over and thank me for helping their coach. I find out that Louis is their assistant offensive coach.

After the guys leave to get ready for their warm-up, I turn and smack into a wall. Well, a wall that smells good and is wearing a suit. OH GOD. I stare at the chest in front of me, having to grab its arm to keep from falling on my ass. My eyes trail up the chest, and then I'm looking into the eyes of the one and only Declan O'Reilly. I start to back up slowly because I feel like I got zapped by the AED that I just used on the Coach.

"Hey, Declan," I hear Dom say as I take another step back. "Great timing! This is my brother, Lorenzo, and my sister, Giovanna. You know the rest of the family." He chuckles as I start to slink away.

Whew! I've successfully made it to stand behind my Papà while I hear Declan greet Enzo. He then steps closer to me to say hi. I'm pretty sure I nod and give him a weird little wave. I feel like my cheeks are on fire and by the look that Enzo is giving me...Yeah, they probably are.

"Is this your first game?" I hear Declan ask me and Enzo.

"It is," Enzo answers and I think I nod again.

I'm pretty sure I've turned into a bobblehead at this point.

Bobble, bobble, bobble.

Declan

I've never seen anyone as beautiful as Giovanna Mancini. Where the hell has Dom been hiding her? We've played together for three years now, and I've never seen or heard anything about him having another brother or a sister. I always thought it was only Sebastiano.

When Giovanna stepped in to save Coach Louis, I couldn't keep my eyes off of her. It was incredible to see her work like that. I need to get to know her. When she turned into me and grabbed my arm, it sent a jolt through my body that I've never felt before. Then she looked at me, and I saw she had the most beautiful green eyes, it was like looking into a kaleidoscope of emeralds. All I heard in my head was *mine*. She's mine. It's crazy.

She bolted out of the locker room like her ass was on fire. I will get her to talk to me. But first we need to play our game, after that I'll have more time to get to know Giovanna.

Giovanna

I practically run out of the locker room and find my way out to the arena. I can see the fans beginning to go through the metal detectors and get their free gift. Tonight's gift is a Hawks blanket. Everyone that comes into the arena will get one until they run out.

I have a smile plastered on my face as I look at the shops with Grady. There's little kiosks all around the United Center on every level. So many cute things that I want to buy. I feel like a kid in a candy store.

I whip my head around as I feel someone come up beside me and turn to see Bastian, Enzo, Rella, Sal, and Luca.

"Where are Mam and Papà?" I ask. Sebastiano chuckles when he sees the bags that Grady is carrying for me. I stick my tongue out at him.

"They went to our seats. Asked us to get them some nachos, hotdogs, and drinks," Rella answers.

There's more than a few fans staring at Bastian, and I giggle. It must be odd for them to see Bastian with us, since he and Dom are identical twins. He's also wearing Dom's jersey.

I stop in the main store, it's pretty big and they have almost every type of merchandise you could want. Jerseys, hats, t-shirts, pants, kids' clothes, stuffed animals, even jewelry. I grab a beanie, a scarf, and a stuffed mascot doll, Benny the Hawk.

"You need a jersey," I tell Grady while I try to spot one that will fit him, which is harder than you would think.

"Why? You want me to blend in more?" He snorts.

Joke's on him though, because I did it. I found a jersey that will fit his gigantic body. "Try this one on."

He grumbles but puts the jersey on over his shirt.

"Yes! I knew it would fit." I pull the tags off and hold onto them while I stand in line.

After I pay for everything, we keep walking and finally see the food booths. There's burgers, chicken fingers, corn dogs, french fries, and beer. Lots of beer. We find the place that sells hot dogs and nachos. They serve the nachos in a plastic hockey helmet—they're cute, and I stand in line to get a few of them. One with jalapeños and two without because jalapeños equal death.

After getting all the food, we're finally ready to head to our seats. Tonight we have glass seats which means we are right next to the Hawks' bench, against the glass.

The minute we walk through the tunnel connecting the shops to the seating area, I'm mesmerized. It's one of the most awesome places I've ever seen. Seeing it on TV does it zero justice. The ice is glistening and the logos painted on it are so vivid. I take a deep breath. You can smell the ice—it's a clean smell, like a new snowfall. I can't stop smiling as we walk down to our seats. We pass out the food as we get settled.

The Hawks come out for their warm-up. Rella waves at Cillian. He smiles and comes over to tap the glass in front of her, then blows her a kiss. Dom skates by, he smiles at all of us as he waves and heads to his net.

"You two are adorable," I say to Rella. We see Declan coming out onto the ice at last. I watch him as he skates by us. He taps the glass in front of me with his stick like Cillian did to Rella. He's so close I can see the gold flecks in his green eyes. And those dimples. God, those dimples. I hear people cheering his name as he smiles at me. I can feel the heat in my cheeks as I raise my hand to wave at him.

Dom frowns from his net, glaring at Declan.

"I think someone has an admirer," Rella teases me.

"Shush." I giggle. I can't take my eyes off Declan while he warms up. He's joking around with the guys, but I can see he's watching me too.

Enea

"I don't like how Declan is looking at our Gia," I whisper to Gráinne.

"I think it's sweet."

I roll my eyes at her dramatically.

"Rella and Cillian are happy. Maybe Declan will be good for Gia. Look at the way she watches him. She likes him," she whispers.

"No. We just got her back and I'm not ready to share her with anyone."

She sighs and kisses my cheek.

"I know, *amore mio*. I know," she says.

Chapter Two

Giovanna

The team leaves the ice and the opening videos start up along with the laser light show. It's amazing, the fans are cheering and I'm captivated by the laser show. I've never seen anything like it, I love being a Hawks fan.

After the laser show ends, the team comes out of their locker room. The crowd roars as they file onto the ice one by one. The starting players take their places as the announcer says to stand for the National Anthem. I get goosebumps when I hear the song start. Hawks fans are known for cheering through the Anthem. The singer tonight is a well known opera singer, Cole Jameson. Hearing it on TV will never compare to hearing him in person.

Watching the Redhawks play live is even better

than I imagined. Watching Declan get his third hat trick of the season was incredible. He also got into a fight when one of the other teams players skated into Dom—always protect your goalie. Two pucks got by Dom, but otherwise he's a beast in the net.

The atmosphere in the arena is deafening, people are screaming and hitting the plexiglass as the Redhawks win against the Boston Bruins, 5-2. As the team skates around the ice, '*Sweet Home Chicago*' starts playing. We all cheer and sing along.

We head back to the locker room after saying goodbye to our parents. We're waiting for Dom and Cillian, along with the wives and girlfriends of the other players. There are also a handful of 'puck bunnies'. They're the girls who will do whatever it takes to get a hockey player to sleep with or fall in love with them. You can always tell who they are. They're the ones in really short dresses, super high heels, and smell like they took a bath in their perfume. The guys start coming out and going over to their wives and girlfriends, waving as they walk past us. After what happened with their assistant coach, I also get a few high-fives. We finally see Dom coming out with Declan and Cillian.

"Shit," I mutter so softly that only Rella hears me. I give Dom a fist bump. "Congrats on the win!"

Declan's smiling as he makes his way towards me. Rella pokes me in the side with her elbow.

"Okay, time to go," Bastian says as he starts to drag me with him.

"Hey! Aren't we going for drinks? We always meet the guys at O'Connor's Pub in Pantherville after a game," Cillian says as he looks at all of us.

Bastian and Enzo say no just as Dom says yes.

Declan chuckles. "Come on, it'll be a good time," he says to my brothers. He turns back to me. "You can ride with me if you want."

Enzo answers for me, "No that's okay, we'll meet you there."

I scowl at him.

Declan looks a little sad but nods. "Okay, I'll see you there."

I grumble at Enzo while I get into the SUV. "You do realize that I'm an adult, right? We're the same age and everything."

"So? We can't just let you go off with some guy," Bastian says.

"Papà would kick our asses if we let you go with him," Enzo adds.

"First of all, he's not 'some guy', he's Dom's teammate. Second, I think I would be perfectly safe riding with him," I grumble some more and look to Dom for help. But he's not saying anything. Well then.

When we get to the pub, we luckily find a parking space close to the entrance.

Declan comes over to our car, opens the door, and takes my hand.

"Is this okay?" he whispers.

I look up at him and smile...I feel that jolt again as I look down at our hands, then back at him. He has the same expression that I do, staring at our intertwined hands. I nod at him as he squeezes my hand.

We walk into the pub and I look around. It's not too loud, surprisingly. I spot a few empty tables and booths. Some of the guys from the team are already at a table, waving at us. We make our way over to them, bringing a few of the tables closer so we can all sit together.

Sebastiano

"Should we stop that?" I ask Enzo quietly, looking at Declan and Gia holding hands.

"Sì." Enzo squeezes between them, forcing Declan to let go of her.

"Seriously?" I hear her snap at Enzo. I hold back a chuckle and watch her try to push him away, but he won't budge.

"Baby!" We hear a woman exclaim. She runs to Declan and plasters herself onto him.

Shit. That's Declan's ex-girlfriend. At least I think she's his ex. I haven't seen her around for a long time. We used to see her every time we went out. I never really liked her, in fact he knows no one really did. We were all so relieved when he said they broke up. Dom said they even cheered in the locker room when they found out.

"I'm so glad I decided to come here tonight! I missed you tons. I'm so sorry I couldn't make it to your game, but I watched it on TV, and you were awesome as usual!"

We watch him turn his head as she tries to kiss him.

"What are you doing, Josephine? Let me go," he growls at her.

She ignores what he said and turns to all of us. "Hi! I'm Josie Reynolds, Declan's girlfriend," she announces to the table.

"You're not my girlfriend. Now leave or I'll have you escorted out," he snaps, standing up and glaring at her.

Giovanna

"I need a drink." I get up and make my way to the bar with Dom and Grady. We order drinks for the whole table and a couple of shots to take right now.

"You okay, Gia?"

"I thought he was single. I mean I heard that he had a girlfriend before, but I thought they broke up."

"He's not lying. It's been at least a year since I've seen her around. But I still don't want you to date him."

I roll my eyes at him. He snickers as I punch him in the arm.

"Maybe they got back together? Anyway, what do I care? All he did was hold my hand." I shrug while we wait for the drinks. I'm lying, of course. I do want Declan, I've never felt that kind of electricity with anyone. My whole body feels like it's on fire when he's near me.

Declan

Josie is my ex. We broke up over a fucking year ago yet she still acts like we're together. Now she's doing it in front of Giovanna. Fuck! Why won't she just stop? We were together for three years, and at the beginning, things were good. I even thought I loved her. But after a while, I realized that I didn't miss her when I was away for games and I didn't look forward to seeing her when I came home. I was stupid to let it go on for so long. I should've ended it the moment I realized how I felt.

I guess I hung onto her because of my fear of being alone. I lost my parents when I was sixteen. They were out for their twentieth anniversary dinner and were hit by a drunk driver, whose blood alcohol concentration was two times the legal limit. My dad died at the scene, and my mom hung on for about a week. She was only conscious for one day and I had to tell her we had lost him. My mom was a strong woman, and she loved me unconditionally. But I think the thought of living her life without my dad, who she always called her soulmate, broke her heart. And in the end she just couldn't do it. They had a love that I can only hope to find one day. I miss them so much.

My parent's best friends—who are also my god

parents—Henry and Carissa Larson took me in after my parents died. Henry was also my high school hockey coach. They have four children of their own, two boys and two girls. We always considered them family so moving in with them made sense. They made sure I kept my grades up and went to practice every day. The day I was drafted by the Chicago Redhawks, they both told me how proud they, and my parents, are of me. Neither of them ever spoke about my parents like they were gone. I've always felt like they're still here with me and I know they would've loved Giovanna.

I wasn't kidding when I said I would have Josie escorted out. Tonight is for getting to know Giovanna. I know deep in my soul that she's the one I've been waiting for.

Giovanna

Josie comes up to stand beside Dom, Grady and me while we wait for our drinks.

"You played great tonight!" she says to Dom.

"Thanks," he mumbles without looking up.

She orders her drink, then turns to me. "I'm Josie." She smirks and offers me her limp hand.

"Giovanna."

"How long have you and Domenico been together?"

I blink a few times. "Dom's my brother," I say slowly.

"Oh! Sorry. You two looked so cozy over here." She waves her hand at me dismissively. "Declan and I have been together for almost four years now."

Wonder why she thinks I need to know all this.

"Wow, that's a long time. You seem happy."

Not Declan, though. He actually looked like he was going to be sick when he saw her.

"Declan's the best. He's my everything," she continues.

I grab the shots and down them with Dom.

When the bartender finally brings us the rest of the drinks, we head back to the table.

"Oh! I'll come with you!" She invites herself.

I roll my eyes at Dom, then walk back to the table and sit down next to Enzo.

Josie tries to sit next to Declan, who moves over by Dom without looking at her. She frowns as she watches Declan move away from her.

Rella downs her shot and part of her beer before she grabs my hand. "Let's go dance."

I chug my drink before she can yank me with her.

While we're dancing, I feel someone come up behind me. I turn and look into the most beautiful pair of green eyes. The way he looks at me makes me feel like I'm the only woman in the room. Then, when he wraps his arms around me, I get that butterfly feeling in my stomach as we sway slowly to the music. I lay my head on his chest and close my eyes.

I peek over at Fiorella and Cillian, who are getting cozy while they dance. I look up at Declan to discover that he's staring at me again.

"You're so beautiful," he whispers.

I shiver slightly, feeling him brush his lips against my ear. "I don't think your girlfriend would like you dancing with me or telling me that I'm beautiful."

He pulls back slightly so I can see his face as he says, "She's not my girlfriend. We haven't been together in a long time."

I look down slightly. "That's not what she said earlier. She says you've been together for four years and that you're the love of her life."

Right as Declan is about to answer me, Josie appears.

"Can I sneak in and dance with my baby?" She glares at me.

I start to let go of Declan, but he doesn't let go of me, so I'm forced to stay where I am.

"No. I'm not yours, Josie. You know damn well that we aren't together. So please stop," Declan says, keeping his arms wrapped around me.

"Why are you saying this, Declan? Cause she's pretty? You're acting like I don't matter now?" she asks loudly and people turn to stare.

I try again to get away from them but Declan is holding on like he's glued to me.

"Please don't go," he whispers in my ear, holding me tighter still.

"I don't want to be in the middle of this."

There's a big part of me that doesn't want to let him go. I listen to it and stay in his arms.

"Declan O'Reilly! Why would you do this to me?" she shrieks while stomping her foot like a petulant child.

Declan and I look at each other.

"I need another drink," I say and he nods. We start to head back to our group.

Josie grabs my arm and tries to slap me, but I duck and stare at her in surprise.

Declan grabs Josie's wrist. "Don't ever touch her," he says, throwing her hand back to her.

Declan

I can't believe Josie tried to hit Giovanna. What the fuck is wrong with her?

I refuse to let Giovanna walk away while I deal with Josie. I know we just met, but I need her to know that she's everything to me, and that I don't want to be alone with Josie for any reason.

I don't know why I feel so strongly about Giovanna. All I know is that I need her.

"Why are you doing this?" I growl angrily at Josie.

"Because I own you, Declan. You belong to me," she declares.

"I don't belong to you or with you. You chose your

path and that path didn't involve me. So this crap that you're trying to pull stops now," I say angrily.

"So I made a teeny-tiny mistake." She shrugs. "I was feeling neglected. I've apologized and now we need to move past it and get on with the life we had planned," she asserts.

I snort. "You're crazy! I will never be with you again. I don't care what you say." I guide Gia back to the table.

Josie tries to grab my arm.

"Don't touch me ever again. Now leave us alone," I say in a low voice, looking her in the eye.

Josie starts to take a step towards us, reaching out to grab me again. Stopping when she sees the look on my face.

Giovanna

"She's crazy!"

"It's been over for more than a year."

"I don't want the drama, Declan. I want to get to know you, but maybe it's not the right time," I say right as he leans in to kiss me. I swear I see fireworks. Everything around us fades away...It's just us. I moan softly feeling his arms pull me in tighter to him.

"I'm not with Josie. She did something that I will never forgive or forget."

I'm about to ask what she did when Josie comes stomping up. Declan's back is to her and I sigh.

"Declan, come here!" she barks at him. I feel him take a deep breath without turning around. "You said we would try. Now that you've met her, you don't want to even look at me." She points at me and she's getting louder. "You think you're special because Declan is paying attention to you? Well you're not. That's how he works. He'll sweet talk you, fuck you and lead you on till he thinks he's found something better, then he'll leave you."

I take a step back. "Look, I don't know what your problem is. Declan said you aren't together and you haven't been for a long time. Yet you insist on making a scene. You've got issues. I'm sorry that you feel like I'm the cause of your problems, but I'm not," I calmly tell her. I feel Declan's hand on my lower back. We walk past her, back towards our table.

"God, that was so fucking sexy." His voice is gravelly as he nips my ear.

I close my eyes as I turn and face him.

Just as I do that, we hear Josie screaming, "I'M PREGNANT, DECLAN O'REILLY!"

We do our best to ignore her. When we rejoin the table, everyone is silent.

Josie has followed us, still yelling about being pregnant.

"Well I hope the father of your child steps up and helps you, Josie. Because we both know that the baby isn't mine." He motions to the bouncer, who makes his way over to us. Declan quietly asks him to have Josie escorted out of the pub.

We all watch as the bouncer asks Josie to leave. When she refuses, he and another bouncer walk her out. She's still yelling about being pregnant with Declan's baby. People are staring and whispering.

I turn to him. "What if she's carrying your child?"

He's shaking his head before I can even get the sentence out.

"I haven't been with with her in like, a year. And I've never, I repeat, never had unprotected sex."

Chapter Three

Giovanna

I go to my second game two nights later with Enzo, Bastian, Sal, Rella and Luca. The Hawks win again, 4-0.

Like the last game, we head back to the locker room area to wait. We make small talk as we wait for Dom, Cillian and Declan to come out. I've been texting with Declan since the night we met.

After each game they either get physical therapy if they're hurting, or work out. Then they shower. So it can be a wait of sometimes up to two hours or more. Thank god there are couches.

The wives and girlfriends that we saw last time smile at us. The puck bunnies are glaring at us. I find it funny that they're always here. I didn't see any of the guys leave with them last time, so I'm wondering why they keep trying. A few of them are staring at Bastian. It looks like they want to come over, I overheard some of them say that they'd take Sebastiano cause he looks just like Domenico. Gross. Then there's Grady and Marco, mine and Rella's bodyguards. Women throw themselves at them too.

"Ew." Rella and I are watching a girl lick her lips while looking at Enzo.

Rella snickers as we continue to watch the girl, who goes as far as pulling her already short skirt up higher.

Enzo slides over to us and whispers, "Save me."

I chuckle at Enzo, who's trying to hide behind Grady. Grady's big body is shaking from laughing.

We see Dom, Cillian and Declan walking out together. Some of the girls try to latch onto them, but they politely decline and head over to us.

"That game was awesome!" I say to my brother as I hug him.

"Do I get a hug too?" I hear Declan ask, coming up beside me.

"Well I don't know, is Josie going to pop out and try to hit me again?" I say while trying to keep a straight face.

"No," he growls at me. He then realizes I'm teasing him because I can't keep from laughing. He laughs too, and hugs me, then takes my hand.

"Okay, let's go," Enzo says.

I look over and read the text Dom's sending to our papà.

> Domenico: Hey Papà, we're going to grab a few drinks with some of the team

> Enea: Okay. Please keep an eye on your sister. And have fun

I roll my eyes at Dom. "I'm a big girl, you know. I can take care of myself."

"Too bad. You'll always be the baby. And Papà's only daughter."

I know what Dom's talking about, the fear that my family has about the kidnapping will never go away. And truth be told? I love that my parents and brothers are so protective of me.

"You want to ride with me?" Declan asks while we're walking to the cars.

"No, she doesn't," Enzo barks as he opens the door and pushes me rudely into our SUV. Declan looks at me as he sighs, then nods at Enzo.

"I'll see you there," he says.

I wave at him.

After my brothers get into the SUV and we head to the pub, I smack Enzo on the arm.

"You should be nicer to Declan. I really like him, and if you screw this up for me, I'm going to be pissed."

"Why? I know who he is. I watch hockey, just like you. I've heard things about the guys. Shit, even Dom has a reputation with women. And look what happened the other night with Josie," he retorts.

Dom glares at Enzo. "Hey, I'm not a player."

"Yes, you are." He glares back.

"No, *fratellino*. I am not a fucking player. I don't touch puck bunnies and I don't sleep with random women. Neither has Declan in the three years we've played together, as far as I know."

Enzo rolls his eyes as Marco parks the SUV.

"Thank you," I say to Grady as he opens the car door for me.

Walking to the pub entrance, we pass people waiting in line. We can hear them whispering to each other when they see Dom, Declan, Cillian and some of their teammates.

Declan takes my hand as the guy at the door gestures at our group and steps aside to let us in. I feel myself blush. He pulls me to his side as we walk to the VIP section.

"I'm really glad you came tonight," Declan whispers in my ear.

"Live music?" Marco asks Dom.

"Yeah, they have random bands come and play. They're usually big names, but they don't announce who it is till they're ready to get onstage."

Grady comes to stand near me. I'm getting used to having him around.

After we grab some drinks and get settled, I hear the music start. I turn to the stage and exclaim to Enzo, "It's Skid Row!"

He chuckles at me as I jump up and rush towards the stage with Grady right behind me.

When I see Rachel Bolan, the bassist and founder of Skid Row, I smile even bigger. Holy hell, is he sexier in person! I've been a fan since I was about thirteen. But this is the first time I've seen them live.

I sing along with the lead singer (he's new and he sounds awesome) as I study Rachel. The song ends and the band announces that they'll be back after a short break.

I follow Enzo and Grady to the bar to get more drinks. There's a commotion behind us, and we glance back to see the band heading our way.

Grady and Enzo close in around me as I spot Rachel. He looks over and smiles. I realize he's walking directly towards us, but his progress is slowed by the hoard of women trying to get his attention.

I chuckle and turn back towards the bar. Then I hear a voice.

"Can I buy you a drink?" I look into the eyes of none other than Rachel Bolan. Kill. Me. Now.

"I, um, I already ordered, but thank you." He's watching me as he grabs the beer the bartender is handing him.

"I'm Rachel."

"I know." I'm pretty sure my cheeks are bright red. I can't believe he's standing in front of me. I spent so many of my teen years drooling over this man.

"Don't you want to tell me your name?" He chuckles.

"Oh sorry!" I laugh. "My name is Giovanna."

"Beautiful woman with an equally beautiful name." He winks.

"Let's go," Enzo says as he and Grady grab our drinks.

"It was nice meeting you!" I say to Rachel.

"Wait! Can we join you?"

"Uh, sure."

When we get back to the group, I introduce Rachel and the rest of the band to everyone.

"So, I noticed you know the all lyrics to our songs," Rachel says, sitting next to me.

"I do. I've been a fan since your first album."

He smiles at me and I see Declan glaring at him out of the corner of my eye.

"So the guys you were with while we were playing, one of them your boyfriend? Husband?" he asks, causing me to giggle.

"No. One is my twin brother and the other is a friend." I hate having to explain who Grady is, so it's just easier to call him my friend.

"You have a lot of guys around you."

Just as I'm about to answer him, Rella sits down.

"Fiorella, Rachel Bolan. Rella is my cousin."

"Nice to meet you," Rachel says to her, smiling and shaking her hand.

Cillian sits next to Rella. "This is Cillian McGregor," she says to Rachel.

"Oh shit! You play for the Hawks!" Rachel

exclaims. He's finally looking around and notices the team surrounding us.

Cillian tilts his head and smiles. "You're a fan?"

"Been a fan all my life," he says as Declan inserts himself between me and Rella, causing her to give him a dirty look.

He ignores her and puts his arm around my waist, pulling me closer to him. I feel my body mold to his.

"Whoa, Declan O'Reilly!" Rachel says, glancing over to where Declan's arm is.

"Rachel, Declan." They shake hands while I finish my drink.

"Dance?" Rachel asks me.

"Sure." I turn to look at Declan as Rachel helps me up. Declan watches us walk towards the dance floor as a slower song starts.

Declan

"Of course it's a slow song," I mutter to myself. I can't keep my eyes off Giovanna.

Fuck. Giovanna is mine. I need her to know that before she starts something with that dude. He's got a fucking chain connecting his nose to his ear for fuck's sake. He's touching her and just as I'm about to lose my shit, I realize Rella is talking to me.

"Shit. Sorry, Rella. What did you say?" I tear my eyes away from Giovanna to look at her.

"I said why don't you go and ask her to dance? Stop being a fucking baby. Make your damn move. I know you like her."

"But maybe she doesn't want me. Especially after that shit with Josie." I frown, watching Rachel whisper something in Gia's ear that makes her laugh.

"You're a fucking moron," Rella says to me.

Cillian snorts and some of his drink dribbles out of his mouth.

I glare at both of them and sigh.

"Well that's attractive," she teases, handing him a napkin. Then giving him a kiss after he's wiped the dribble off his chin.

I keep watching Gia while listening to Fiorella and Cillian talk. Finally, I see Rachel and Giovanna walking off the dance floor. I quickly stand up and go over to her, pushing my way past Rachel.

I grab her hand. "Come dance with me?" She looks at me and lets me lead her back to the dance floor. I grin as I see Rachel frown, then turn and head back to our group.

"You're so damn beautiful," I say, holding her as close as I can.

"Thank you."

That smile she's giving me? Yup, I'm done. I hold her even tighter as another slow song starts. I feel her lay her head on my chest and she lets out a soft sigh. I could stay like this forever. In fact that is exactly what I plan on doing—holding her forever.

Giovanna

I'll admit, dancing with Rachel was nice. But being in Declan's arms? It feels like home. I don't know if I can keep my distance anymore. I obviously don't want to deal with his ex because she's crazy, but I want Declan. I reluctantly let go of him when the music changes, and we head back to the VIP section.

I sit down next to Rella and watch Declan give Rachel a death stare.

Rella laughs as she pokes me in my side.

"Declan was going nuts when you were dancing with Rachel," she whispers.

"Why? We were just dancing. And besides, Declan and I aren't together," I whisper back just as Rachel gets up.

"I hope we can hang out after we finish our set," he says to all of us.

"That would be nice." I get up and follow him to the stage. Dom and Grady come with me.

"You know your friend is always following you, right?" Rachel says as he looks over at Grady.

I chuckle. "I know, it's okay."

He nods, then goes backstage with his band.

I feel someone come up behind me. It's like I just know when Declan is near me, but I turn to make sure anyway. "Hi."

"I didn't want you to be up here alone," he says as he leans over and kisses me lightly.

"She's not alone," Grady says from beside me and I roll my eyes.

We spend the rest of the night dancing and hanging out with Skid Row. Easily one of my best nights ever.

Chapter Four

Giovanna

Lorenzo and I had decided to take a month off from school to deal with everything that's been going on. But now we're headed back to Crimson. It's been quite an adjustment. Hearing Dorian admit to what he did made it easier for me to accept being back with our real family.

"LORENZO AONGHUS MANCINI! Are you ready yet? I won't be late for my first day back because you're slow!" I hear one of our older brothers laughing. "What are you laughing about?" I snipe, turning to see Domenico.

"Because he's already in the boat." He laughs louder as he points to the dock. I look outside to see

Enzo waving from the boat, grinning like the Cheshire Cat.

"Ugh. Fucking asses. Both of you." Pointing at them, I stick my tongue out and stomp out to the pier.

"Language," our mam says as I stomp past her.

"Sorry, Mam!" I smack Dom who's still snickering at me.

Now that we're back in school, we live on Lucciola Island. There are two other houses on our tiny island along with ours. To get to Crimson, it's a short fifteen minute boat ride, then a twenty minute drive.

"Hey, Giovanna!" I hear someone yell as we're walking to class, and I turn to see my brother Jérôme running towards us. He grabs me and twirls me around. I have to put my hand out to stop Grady from attacking him.

"Hi!" I giggle as he's swinging me around. We hear Dom clear his throat and Jérôme puts me down.

"Dom, Grady, this is Jérôme. Jérôme, this is Dom and Grady."

"Boyfriend?" Dom and Jérôme say at the same time as they frown.

"No, ew! You're both my brothers...and Grady." I look between all of them. They eye each other while Grady stands with his arms crossed, making him look bigger.

Dom is about five inches taller and probably forty pounds heavier than Jérôme, but that doesn't stop Jérôme from staring right back at him.

"What are you doing here? Are you alone?" I ask

Jérôme. He shakes his head no, and I see my other three brothers heading over. I run to hug each of them.

"This is Christophe, Fabian and François. This is Dom and Grady," I introduce my brothers and Grady to each other. It's a little awkward because to me they're all my brothers, blood or not. Christophe nods at Dom.

"We miss you," François says, tearing up.

Enzo comes running up and hugs them too.

"I miss you too," I whisper, hugging François tighter.

"Papa really misses you both," Christophe says softly.

"That bastard is not their father," Dom snarls through clenched teeth.

Moving closer to Dom, I put my hand on his arm, then look at Christophe. "I know he does, Chris, but I just can't."

"We can't," Enzo echoes softly, stepping up next to Dom and me.

"Can we have dinner together? Please?" Fabian asks, looking at us, then at Dom.

"Of course we can. How about Friday night, 7pm at the Seaside Bistro?" I suggest.

"Papà won't let you two go alone," Dom says in a gentle voice to me.

"I know. I was hoping you, Bastian, Mam, and Papà will come too," I respond.

"I'll call them while you're in class."

I kiss his cheek.

"Grazie. Okay, I'm going to be late if I don't go now." I look at all of them. "I will never choose between you, you're all my brothers."

"I'll walk you to class," Fabian says. I take his arm and Grady follows us.

Domenico

"He won't hurt her," Enzo says to me as we watch Gia walk away with one of the Laurents.

"I know. I missed twenty-three years of being your big brother. I'm just a little jealous." I sigh.

"I understand," Enzo says. "I'll see you after class." He turns and heads to his class.

After Gia and Enzo leave, I'm left with the damn Laurent boys. Well, most of them.

"I wanted to say I'm sorry for what my father did," Christophe says. "I can't imagine what your family went through when you lost the twins. Not having them around is killing me. I understand how much this has hurt you and your parents. But please know that we protected them with our lives. We love them with everything in us. Even my father. I know you'll never forgive him, but he loves them just as much as he loves us." He's holding back his emotions, but all I can do is stare at him.

"I don't blame you or your brothers. But I'll never forgive your father. There's nothing he could ever say that would make what he did alright. Has he said why he took them? Or why he didn't just give them back?"

He shakes his head. "I wish I knew. All he says is that it was a war and he never intended to hurt them. He just wanted to hurt your dad."

"I'll talk to my parents about dinner. But your father better not show up or I'll make sure you never see or speak to Gia or Enzo again."

"He won't. Thank you, we miss them so much."

I shake his hand and he turns to leave with his brothers.

I sigh and call my parents to tell them about the dinner. They agree to it, we just have to work out when. I know Gia wanted to do it this weekend, but Papà can't be there because of work.

Even though Grady is always with Gia, today I want to be there too. That damn Dorian took so much from us when he kidnapped them. He didn't just hurt my parents, he hurt Bastian and me too. I remember the day they were taken. My mother stopped talking to everyone for a long time. She locked herself in her room and just cried.

Giovanna

I'm really excited that we're going to have dinner with my Laurent brothers. I want my parents, Bastian and Dom to get to know them. No matter what Dorian did, my brothers were babies then and had no knowledge of what happened. I know it'll be hard for them at first, but in time they'll like each other.

I finish my last class of the day and go to meet Dom. I see Declan standing with him, and there's a bunch of girls surrounding them. Well fine, there are guys there too, but still. When Declan sees me, his face lights up with the biggest smile.

"How was your day?" Dom asks.

"Insightful," I say blandly. I look at Declan who's inching closer to me, even though some girl is trying to get his attention.

He finally makes it over to me and gives me a hug. "Hi beautiful," he says as he kisses my cheek.

"Hi." I smile up at him. "What are you doing here?" I ask as Enzo joins us.

"Dom said that he was coming to visit you and I've never been to Crimson. He invited me to come out, so I got on a plane this morning. When I got here, he said he was waiting for you to finish your classes, so I came to see you...I mean I came to keep Dom company." He chuckles as we see Dom making a face. "I'll head back to Chicago with him on Friday."

"You're a dick." Dom laughs at Declan.

Declan has his arm around me. I notice the girls aren't liking this too much. Oh well.

"So Declan, you didn't answer me about dinner tonight," one of the girls says to him.

"Sorry, I can't," he says, smiling at me, then looking at Dom for help.

"Uh yeah, sorry. We have plans."

"Well, what about this weekend?" she pushes.

I turn my face into Declan's chest and snicker. So many of them just don't give up. Most times it's frustrating, but days like today? It's just funny.

"I have a function this weekend," he says, tightening his hold on me.

"I could go with you," she says.

"I already have a date, but it was nice of you to offer. I don't live here, and I have to head home," he says, tightening his hold on me.

"You could fly me to Chicago and I can hang out with you," she says coyly. She keeps trying to touch his arm.

He is staring at her like she has two heads. "I don't think I can do that."

Wait, he has a date? I feel his arms tighten more as I try to pull away.

"We should get going!" Enzo blurts out.

"It was nice talking with you all." Dom waves at the group and we start to walk away.

"Wait! You didn't give me your number!" the girl yells at Declan.

"Keep walking, man. Not worth it." Dom's snickering at him.

"Wow! That girl just won't give up." Enzo laughs.

Declan won't let go of my hand as we walk.

"So you have a date this weekend?" I ask, trying not to sound jealous.

"No. I just said that to make her stop. Unless you're going out with me."

I shake my head. "I can't, I have to study."

"When will you be back in Chicago?"

"Not till next Friday."

I see his chest heave as he takes a deep breath.

"And then I'll be back the following weekend for the Charity Date Auction."

Declan looks puzzled for a minute. "Is that the thing I missed last year?" He looks at Dom.

"Yep. Same one. You gonna let us auction you off this year?"

The look on Declan's face makes me snicker.

"I'm going to say no." He laughs. "I heard the stories from last time."

Dom shudders. "Fuck, man. It was brutal. That girl tried to eat me alive on our date. We only made it to the restaurant—she wanted to get drinks after and I had to have Bastian call and give me an excuse to leave!" We all laugh as he looks at us like he's still traumatized.

"And you want me to agree to be auctioned off?" Declan guffaws. "No thanks."

Chapter Five

Declan

I loved surprising Gia last week at her school. Enea invited me to stay on the island with them for the few days I was there. It was so hard to leave.

I've also been dealing with Josie. Because of her public outburst, there's a lot of rumors going around about the pregnancy and the baby being mine. I know for a fact that it isn't, and I wish she would just move the fuck on. I'll never understand why she won't.

Declan: Good morning, beautiful! Are you finally going to let me take you out to dinner?

Giovanna: LOL. You're not going to give up, are you?

Declan: Never. I would chase you
around the world

Giovanna: How are things with Josie?

I puff out a breath in exasperation. I knew the situation still bothered her. Fuck, it bothers me. I'm one hundred percent sure that if Josie is pregnant, the baby isn't mine. If she had gotten pregnant the last time we had sex, the baby would be three months old by now. But I don't know how to reassure Gia that there's nothing that could make me leave her and go back to Josie.

Declan: I haven't spoken to her since
that night at the pub. She's lying about
me being the father

Giovanna: So the charity auction this
weekend that Dom was talking about?
The proceeds go to Lucciola Memorial
Hospital. If you're interested, I can get
you as many tickets as you need

Well shit, I guess she isn't going to respond to the Josie issue? Dammit. I need her to understand that I'm done with that part of my life. In fact, Gia is the first woman I've even wanted to date after all that bullshit with Josie. I guess I'll have to show her instead of telling her. They say actions speak louder than words, right?

Declan: What is being auctioned
besides Dom and some of the guys?

> Giovanna: Every year we get different
> celebrities to help out, professional
> athletes, and even my family. This year
> I'm part of the auction…

My eyes widen as I read her text. This is my chance. She can't say no to a date if I bid and win. I'm not above buying her time. And I'll be damned if any other man is going to put their hands on my woman. I don't need to be going to jail for breaking some poor guy's arms because he was dumb enough to buy a date with my Gia.

> Declan: Does Dom have the team
> covered for tickets?

Last year Dom was auctioned off and the woman who bought him wouldn't stop touching him, he said she even tried to lick him during dinner. Gross. Some of the team helped out at the last auction too. Some of the stories they told were hilarious, but most of them really did have a great time.

> Giovanna: As far as I know, Dom
> hasn't given any tickets to the team
> yet. I know some are coming, because
> they're part of the auction

> Declan: I wasn't able to go last year
> because I had a different function that
> night. Were you there?

> Giovanna: No, I wasn't

I've been wondering where she's been. Dom joined

the team the same time as Cillian and me. Rella started coming around about a year after that.

> Declan: Am I allowed to bid on you?
> (smiling emoji)

> Giovanna: LOL. Maybe. I mean I'm hoping at least one person bids on me (fingers crossed emoji)

She's so damn adorable.

> Declan: I'm sure more than one person will bid on you. In fact I know there will be more than one

> Giovanna: Lol you don't know that. Unless you're a fortune teller. Can you see the future?

> Declan: I can. Do you want to know what I see?

> Giovanna: Of course I want to know what the future holds (crystal ball emoji)

> Declan: I see you finally saying yes to dinner with me and it will be the best dinner date either of us has ever been on

> Giovanna: OH really? What if your future knowledge is wrong? (thinking emoji)

> Declan: Impossible. We're destined to be together

Giovanna

This man is something else. Everything in me wants to say yes to dinner. But what would he think of me if he knew about my past? Then there's the part about my papà being the head of the Chicago mafia. There are always rumors about the Mancini family that surface when Dom's in the news. He usually just stays quiet and lets them talk.

I'm afraid that my new-found insecurities after finding out about being kidnapped have changed me. I used to be so sure of myself and my choices. But now I feel like I don't have control over anything. Because everything I thought I knew about myself and my family was a lie.

I don't want Declan to think I'm weak because of what I fear now. Sometimes I feel like I'm being sucked into a black hole. It's suffocating and I wish I knew how to stop it. There's also the situation with Josie telling everyone that she's pregnant with Declan's baby. He swears there's no possible way it's his. I do believe him, but it's still stressful.

Trust is a hard one for me lately. I want to trust Declan because he hasn't given me any reason not to. He could be the best thing that has ever happened to me. I know that when I'm around him, it feels like that's where I'm supposed to be. That he's what I've been waiting for.

He says he'll be at the charity auction. It should be a fun weekend. Maybe what I'm supposed to do will become clearer then.

Declan

As I wait for Gia to answer me, I get ready to go to the gym. I wish she would just let me take her out. I don't know what it is, but the night I saw her at the game, I just knew I had to have her. Watching her save Coach Louis blew my mind, she was so calm. Then, when I went to see her at school? She stole my heart, I don't even see any other women but her. I don't want anyone but her. I'll win the bid for her, I don't care how much it costs. I'll pay any amount to have her all to myself because I know once I get her alone, she'll see how perfect we are for each other.

I've never been so desperate to be with someone. I've never had to try, girls come with being a professional hockey player. But I won't sleep with just anyone. In fact, I've had very few one night stands. I like being with someone, having someone cheer for me during games. To have that person be there when I come home from away games. Someone to cuddle with when I've had a shit game. I know Gia's the one I've been waiting for.

Declan: Did I scare you?

I text her after I haven't heard back from her in about an hour. I see the three dots pop up so I know she's typing something.

> Giovanna: No, you didn't scare me. In fact I wonder if I'll scare you when you really get to know me

What could have happened for her to feel like that? I don't think there's anything she could say that would make me walk away from her.

> Declan: There is nothing you could say that would scare me away. Ever

> Giovanna: If you say so. Will you be coming to the auction?

> Declan: Definitely. I have to bid on you. I can't let someone else win a date with you before I can take you out

> Giovanna: Lol. You're crazy, Declan O'Reilly

> Declan: Can I see you tonight? We have practice, you could come down with Dom? Or come and work out with me

> Giovanna: I can come with Dom to practice. Are people allowed to watch?

> Declan: Yeah, there will be fans there as well. Usually not too many because it's a night practice, but there are always some

Giovanna: Okay, I'll come and watch you practice. I'm sure Rella will come too. I'll see you tonight. Have a good day

Declan: Have a good day, beautiful. I can't wait to see you

Chapter Six

Giovanna

My parents have been staying on the island with us for the past few weeks. Dom arrived a few days ago, but can only stay for another two because of hockey.

We had planned to have dinner with my Laurent brothers the week they came to see us at Crimson, but we couldn't get our schedules to sync. So here we are, three weeks later and we're all finally able to go to dinner together.

I'm a little nervous about my parents meeting my Laurent brothers. I want them to like each other because I will not be made to choose between them. My Laurent brothers did nothing wrong. That's on Dorian and Nadia, they made that decision for all of us.

I'm surprised that we never came into contact with

any of my Mancini family sooner. I mean it's not like we lived at opposite ends of the country—we were only a few hundred miles away from each other.

For twenty-three years we never bumped into them. Then one day while walking around a mall in another state, we meet. Life is crazy.

I'm almost finished getting ready when Lorenzo comes into my room.

"Are you okay?" I ask him as he sits on my bed. He looks so sad and I hate seeing my twin sad.

"I'm just so confused. Everything we knew and trusted was a lie." I can hear the pain in his voice. "And I was thinking, how did Christophe not know? He was five, Fabien and François were four, and Jérôme was three. They had to wonder, right? Where did they think we came from?" He frowns.

"I don't know, Enzo. We can ask them tonight. I wish Nadia was still here so we could ask her too. If she hadn't died in the accident, would her conscience have made her give us back?"

Enzo gets up and stands next to me, looking at me in the mirror. "I wish we had more answers. But until we're ready to talk to Dorian, we'll never know. I'm so glad I have you, because I don't know if I could do this alone," he says softly.

"It's always been us, Enzo." I say, hugging him. Growing up, we always knew no matter what, we had each other. This is no different, we'll find a way to get through this. "Tonight we'll ask Chris the questions that we have. We just have to remember that whatever they were told, they were kids too. What could they have done even if they knew the truth?"

"I don't think there's anything they could've done. Only Dorian and Nadia had the ability to fix things," Enzo replies.

Because of everything that's happened, I find myself second-guessing things I thought I was sure of. Like, am I really who I think I am? I chose to become a doctor because of losing Nadia. What would I have done if we hadn't been kidnapped?

I think back to when we lost her. She was in a car accident. They tried to save her but they couldn't. In becoming a doctor, I felt like maybe I could save someone else's mamma.

It's time to go. Enzo walks downstairs with me to where our parents and brothers are putting on their jackets. I smile watching them. I miss the Laurents so much, but I love my family.

Grady is in the driver's seat this time when we get into the car. We also have Arturo with us because he's my mam's bodyguard.

It takes about thirty minutes to get to the restaurant and it's pretty quiet in the car the whole way there.

We all get out and leave the car with the valet.

"Thank you for saying yes to this dinner," I say to my parents. "I know this can't be easy, but I want you to know our Laurent brothers."

"I know, *mi passerotta*," my papà says, kissing my head. My papà has started calling me his little sparrow. He says it's what he called me when I was a baby.

"We also know they aren't to blame for any of this," my mam says.

I turn and hug her tight.

"Mancini party of eleven," my papà says to the hostess.

She smiles at him. "Your table will be ready in a few minutes. You can wait here or at the bar if you like."

"Thank you," he says.

I see Christophe first and wait for them all to come into the restaurant. I introduce everyone, then hug my brothers. My papà and brothers shake hands, then they give my mam hugs. So far so good, I think to myself as I smile.

"Your table is ready, if you'll follow me," the hostess says. She leads us to a table with a view of the Sears Tower. It's one of my favorite landmarks in Chicago. It's now the Willis Tower, but to me it will always be the Sears Tower.

We order drinks and appetizers. The silence gets a little uncomfortable.

"I'd like to say how sorry we are for what our father did," Fabien says as the others nod.

"I have a question. How old were all of you when Lorenzo and Giovanna were taken?" my papà asks them.

"I was five, Fabien and François were four, and Jérôme was three," Christophe says. "I know what you're thinking. How did we not know they weren't our real siblings?"

My parents look at all of them, nodding their heads.

"What were you told to make you not question who they were or why they were there? Didn't they cry and ask for us? And why did your parents keep their real names?" my mam asks.

"To be honest, I did ask those questions. My dad told me that they'd lost their parents and it was our job to take care of them from then on. I never questioned it after that. And when they would cry or ask for you, we would tell them that you were in heaven and we were their family now. Eventually, they stopped asking," Chris explains.

"And their names? My dad first told us their names were Olivier and Amélie. But when we called them that, they refused to answer so he said that their middle names were Lorenzo and Giovanna. So we could call them that instead," François says. I can tell that he sees the sadness in my mam's eyes. "I'm so sorry."

"It's not your fault. It's your father's. What was your mother's name?" my father asks.

"Nadia. Her name was Nadia. She was from Sicily and was the one who taught us Italian. When she heard Lorenzo and Giovanna say words in Italian, she made sure to keep speaking to them in Italian. My father was the one who taught us French. Before she died, my mamma made our dad promise to keep talking to us in both languages. When I think about it now, it was probably her way of making sure Lorenzo and Giovanna never really lost what you gave them," Chris says, his voice catching.

"We taught them Italian first. We were starting to teach them Gaelic when they were taken," my mother says, her Irish accent coming out a little stronger.

"You should know that we'll never blame you boys. You couldn't have done anything even if you knew the real reason your father took our babies. Because when he said he found them alone and crying? That is a lie. My children were never left alone. Especially at that time, because there was a lot of conflict between our families," my papà explains.

They nod in understanding.

"We'll never force our dad on any of you. We just want to be able to see Lorenzo and Giovanna. We miss them so much," Jérôme says, looking down and sniffling.

My papà smiles slightly. "You boys are welcome to come to our town anytime. To visit or to stay, if you'd like. We're having our annual Charity Date Auction next weekend, maybe you would like to join us for it?"

"That would be really nice," Jérôme says, giving Enea a big smile. "Thank you!"

"I'll book you rooms at our hotel for the weekend. The auction is on Saturday night, so I'll make your reservations for Friday through Sunday. If you want to stay longer, just let me know."

We spend the rest of dinner talking and having a great time. My Laurent brothers tell stories about Enzo and I as we grew up. They even brought pictures to share with everyone.

When we walk back to the cars after dinner, my

mam hugs each of them. "Thank you for telling us all those stories about them as children. And thank you for taking care of them like you did. I'm really glad they had such a good childhood with you boys." She tears up. "I will treasure these pictures forever."

"You're very welcome. I only wish we could take away the pain that my parents caused you," Fabian says softly.

We all hug each other goodbye and watch the Laurent boys drive off.

"Thank you for tonight," I say to my parents.

"They're good boys," my papà says, hugging me. We get in the car to head home.

Chapter Seven

Giovanna

Have you ever been tricked into doing something? Yeah, that's what happened to me. And the only reason I haven't backed out is because it's for charity. All the proceeds from tonight will go to the hospital here in our little town.

Okay fine, I wasn't really tricked, but my family definitely didn't tell me that I was going to be one of the people up on stage being bid on when they brought this up. They just said I would be 'helping out'. I probably should've asked more questions. Rella is being auctioned off this year too. We're surprised that our papàs agreed to this because they're really protective of us. I asked my papà why he's letting me do this and he said because it's for the hospital. If it wasn't, there's no way he would be okay with it.

Every year they've had quite a few celebrities including teammates of both Domenico and Gianluca —they're the ones that fetch the highest amounts. This year we even have a few firefighters and policemen.

Papà held to his promise about my Laurent brothers being able to join us for the auction. Everyone has a room at the hotel we own, The Legacy. But first, we brought them to Lake Renegade to show them around and to have dinner at our home. After dinner, we head back into the city and to our favorite pub, O'Connors. Tomorrow night, they'll watch us all get auctioned off...yay.

The auction is being held at our hotel. They've transformed the ballroom into an elegant fantasyland. The windows are covered in deep burgundy drapes, the tablecloths are snow white, and there are centerpieces on each table—strands of crystals cascading over white lilies and multi-colored tulips.

"Hi, everyone!" says Cherie, our Master of Ceremonies. "First of all, I want to thank you for coming to our 7th annual Charity Date Auction! If this is your first time here, I'll explain how this works. And if you've done this before, you'll see some familiar faces that are here every year."

Everyone claps and cheers.

"Now for the auction rules. You'll be bidding on a person. Every person is over the age of twenty-one, and dinner and drinks are included in your date." She smiles. "You must pay in full tonight or the next highest bid will win instead. There's no maximum amount that you can bid. Remember, all proceeds go to Lucciola Memorial Hospital."

The crowd cheers and claps more.

"My papà isn't going to like this dress," I mutter to Rella.

She looks at me, then at her own dress. "I think my papà picked my dress out," she says, making a face at it. Being the only two females in our family besides our mothers makes our papàs and brothers, even our uncles, a little protective. Then add in what happened to me as a baby...well you can see where this is going.

"You look beautiful, Gia," Rella says with a smile.

"You always look beautiful, Rella, but you know my papà." I sigh again, stepping out of the dressing room.

"Oh hell no," Bastian says loudly when he sees me. "You can't go out in that." He tries to cover me up with his jacket as he, Dom and Enzo surround me. I knew this was going to happen.

"No. Just. No," Enzo says as he also takes his suit jacket off to put over my shoulders.

"Stop it, Enzo!" I know it's a lot but does he think I'm going to go out there all covered up?

"Why is Rella's dress normal and yours looks like it's missing pieces?" Dom asks angrily.

Sal snickers. "Because we're smarter than you, *cugino*. We picked Rella's dress out ourselves when it was decided she would be doing this," he says, adjusting his shirt and smirking.

"We told you to come with us," Luca says.

Bastian flips Sal and Luca off, scowling at them.

"I didn't choose the dress. It's what I have, so tough shit," I say to my brothers just as our dad comes backstage to check on us.

"What is that?" He points at my dress.

My uncle Leo smiles as he kisses the top of Rella's head. "I told you to come with me, fratello. You said they would pick something nice and tasteful so you didn't have to." He snorts.

Cherie comes running. "Is something wrong? Oh my gosh! You're both stunning," she says smiling at Rella and me.

"She can't go out there in that," my dad says to Cherie as he points at me. "It's not even a whole dress. It's missing pieces!"

The back of my dress is open down to the top of my ass, and dips low in the front. Now, I rarely wear dresses, but I kind of like this gown, and I make the mistake of saying that out loud. Oops.

"What did you just say?" my papà turns slowly to me.

"This gown is perfect," I say, a little too snippy for my papà's taste.

"First, don't talk to me like that. EVER. Second, you're mi passerotta. I've the right to say whatever I want. Third, no."

Cherie looks like she's going to cry. "Enea...I told you about the gown. You said you didn't need to see it," she says nervously.

The room had cleared out the minute my papà stomped in. I can see the crew hiding around the corner and peeking in the doorway as my mam comes over. Cowards.

"What's going on? You look beautiful, amore." She smiles and kisses my cheek. "You look stunning too, baby," she says to Rella.

"That's not a dress, Gráinne, it's not covering enough," he barks at our mam.

Oh. There's also a slit on the left side all the way up to my upper thigh. Maybe it's a bit much, but I really do love this dress. It makes me feel pretty.

"She can't go out like that," Bastian says, looking at our mam.

"This is why I said she shouldn't do this," Dom growls.

"You're not my husband. You're my brothers, you have ZERO say in what I do." I glare at all of them.

"But I do have a say, and I say no," my papà says angrily.

Cherie looks at him wide-eyed. "W-we d-don't have any other o-options," she stutters.

"It's okay, Cherie," our mam says as she puts her hand on Cherie's arm.

Cherie visibly relaxes as she nods.

"You go and take care of what you need to. I can handle grumpy bear over here," she says looking at my papà.

"Baby—" she starts to say to my papà.

"No, amore. She won't go out there like that. Look at her."

Enzo is trying to get his jacket over my shoulders again.

"Stop!" I snap, swatting him away.

My uncles Antonio and Aiden comes back to join us.

"No." Dom comes at me with his jacket from the front this time, while Bastian and Enzo box me in from both sides.

"FOR FUCK'S SAKE! GET THE FUCK OFF ME!" I yell.

"Watch your damn mouth," my papà says in a low voice.

I back down and mumble something unintelligible. I sneak a look at him knowing that I may have pushed him a little too much.

"Enea, stop," I hear my mam say as she puts her hand on his chest. "We're all here with her. She'll be just fine."

He looks at our mam and slowly shakes his head no.

We hear Cherie starting the auction.

"Dom, escort your mother back to her seat and come right back."

Mam sighs as she slowly follows my brother out to our table in the ballroom. My papà takes my arm and leads me to another room. He closes the door and takes a deep breath, then turns to me.

I back up against the wall as I watch him. I've never

seen my papà this mad, except maybe the day we met at the mall.

"Papà—" I start to say as he silences me with a look.

"I'm going to say this once, Giovanna Mancini," he says through his teeth.

"You are mi passerotta. My last born child, my only daughter. But you will never. Ever. Speak to me in that way again in public. EVER." He starts to pace, it's a small room and he's a big man.

"I-I'm sorry, Papà," I whisper. I hear him take another deep breath. Then I feel his arms around me. I melt into them and breathe a sigh of relief.

"I know you want more freedom. But you know how dangerous that is for you. I can't take that chance with you, baby. Not after what's already happened." His voice catches as he holds me tighter. "I can't lose you again."

I know that the men in our family feel that they need to protect the women at all times. Enzo and I being taken as babies only made that worse for my papà. I had more freedom when I was with Dorian, so it's hard to change. But I do understand where my papà is coming from. I know that his biggest fear is losing one of us for good.

I hold him tight as I sniffle. "I'm sorry, Papà. I just got so frustrated."

"I know you are, mi passerotta." He kisses my head.

"I didn't mean to disrespect you. Do you really hate my dress?" I sniffle softly as he lets go of me and looks at the dress again.

"It just shows too much, baby. Maybe we can cover up more in the front, and a little higher in the back? *Per favore.*"

"Okay, Papà. There was a seamstress helping us get ready. She said she can do any alterations that we need."

"Grazie. I love you, mi passerotta."

I kiss his cheek. "I love you too, Papà." He takes my hand and we go back out.

"There's the seamstress. I'll get her and have her fix my dress."

He stands on the side to wait.

"I need you to alter the front and the back of the dress to be a little less revealing, please," I say to the seamstress.

"Are you okay?" Rella asks me.

"I'm okay. I apologized. I know I was out of line. But it's just not fair that the boys don't have to worry about clothes like we have to," I say softly. Rella tries to understand that I grew up differently than she did. Because of what happened to Enzo and me, the rest of them were extremely sheltered. Being the only girl, Fiorella got the worst of it.

"I know, Gia. But I've never seen your papà that mad."

"It'll take me twenty minutes to do the alterations," the seamstress says as I change out of the dress.

"Thank you." I sit with Rella and listen to the auction going on in the ballroom.

"Okay, so far we've had some really great bids!"

Cherie says. "Are you all ready for the Mancini family?" She laughs when the crowd goes wild. "We are going to start with the oldest and work our way down to the youngest."

"First, we have Leonardo Mancini. He's the oldest of the Mancini triplets, six foot five, and COO of Mancini Legacy Enterprises."

He walks out and the ladies start whistling and cheering.

Cherie laughs. "Okay, let's start the bidding at five hundred," she says.

My aunt Rosaura quickly yells, "Ten thousand!"

We hear a few women groaning as Cherie says, "SOLD! And before you get too upset, that is Mrs. Rosaura Mancini, the Mrs. to Leonardo's Mr." She chuckles. Uncle Leo winks at Aunt Rosaura before he walks off the stage to give her a kiss.

"Next we have Enea Mancini. He's the middle triplet, six foot seven, and CEO of Mancini Legacy Enterprises." She laughs, winking at my mam.

"Let's start him at five hundred as well!"

"Ten thousand!" my mam yells, jumping up.

"SOLD! To Mrs. Gráinne Mancini!" She chuckles when more of the women groan and start to grumble about my mother winning in one bid. Cherie laughs more as my papà jumps off the stage and stalks over to my mam. He picks her up and kisses her passionately. The women in the ballroom start to fan themselves.

"Okay you two, calm down. You're making everyone jealous. Enea and Gráinne have been together since high school. Leonardo and Enea help us with our auction to raise money—not for the dates," she teases.

"But the baby triplet—Antonio—is single, ladies!" She smiles as the women cheer. The cheers get louder when he walks out onto the stage. "He's six foot six and CFO of Mancini Legacy Enterprises. Yes, the triplets all work together. Let's start the bidding at five hundred, ladies—and go!" She laughs as the bidding frenzy commences.

"SOLD! For seven thousand to Miss Melody Kent!"

Antonio smiles as he heads over to Melody. He kisses her hand and sits down next to her.

"Next, we have a special bachelor. He is a five-time MotoGP champion. In case you don't know what that is, it's a motorcycle racing championship. And damn, is he sexy. He's six feet tall and the older brother of Gráinne Mancini, Mr. Aiden O'Connor. We'll start his bidding at five hundred!"

The women start screaming bids and we laugh at my uncle who's turning beet red. "Nine thousand going once, going twice, SOLD! To Miss Scarlett Daniels!"

Aiden steps off the stage and walks over to Scarlett. He kisses her hand, then sits down next to her.

"Last year we got to auction off two of Leonardo and Rosaura's children—Salvatore and Gianluca, and the elder twins of Enea and Gráinne—Sebastiano and Domenico. This year we not only have them, but also Leonardo and Rosaura's daughter, Fiorella, and the younger twins of Enea and Gráinne—Lorenzo and Giovanna!" She claps and everyone cheers.

"The next generation of Mancinis will have a reserve price of two fifty. Let's get Salvatore up here! He's six foot three and just graduated from Chicago Police Academy—and go!" Cherie smiles as the women start bidding. "SOLD! To Amanda Markus for seven thousand five hundred."

"Next is Gianluca. He's the third baseman for the Chicago Panthers—six foot four and just adorable. And go!" Cherie laughs at the women screaming. "Okay, nine thousand going once, going twice, SOLD! To Genevieve Carson."

Luca jumps down, fist bumps all the guys, and heads over to Genevieve.

"Next up we have Sebastiano. He's six foot five and is currently getting his Master's degree in IT while working as the Head of Internet Security for Mancini Legacy Enterprises." Women start cheering as Bastian comes out. "Two fifty—and go!" Women start bidding like crazy as Bastian chuckles. "SOLD! For nine thousand to Miss Samantha Darling."

Bastian smiles as he walks off the stage and heads over to Samantha.

"Now we have Sebastiano's twin brother Domenico. By the way, did I mention they were identical?" She laughs. "Domenico is the starting goalie for the Chicago Redhawks, he's number 99 and is six foot five. Let's start the bidding!" Dom smiles as he struts around. "Wow! Nine thousand five hundred going once, twice, SOLD! To Miss Josephine Reynolds!"

Dom pastes on a fake smile when he hears her name. He walks stiffly over to stand near her, but makes sure he's not touching her.

"Ladies and gentlemen, the only daughter of Leonardo and Rosaura Mancini, the beautiful Fiorella! She is currently getting her Fashion Degree at Wildcat University." Rella steps out. "Isn't she gorgeous? Okay, let's start at two fifty!"

Guys start bidding as her brothers and papà give each of them death stares. I cheer from my hiding spot as I watch the bidding. It looks like Cillian is going to win, but the next bid tops his at ten thousand.

The highest bid is now twelve thousand, Rella is smiling as she hears me cheering and tries not to laugh. I look over at my Uncle Leo. He looks like he's going to pop a vein in his neck. I can see my papà snickering at him.

The bidding finally stops as I giggle in my hiding spot.

"SOLD to Mr. Cillian McGregor for thirteen thousand!" Rella smiles while my uncle continues to glare at Cillian. Which makes me laugh harder because even though they've been together for two years, my uncle still gives him death stares. Cillian goes up to the stage and helps her down.

"We are now down to the last two of the night. They are the younger twins of Enea and Gráinne—Lorenzo and Giovanna. Let's start with Lorenzo, who is six foot five and a student at Crimson getting his law degree."

Enzo walks onto the stage and the women start screaming bids before Cherie can say go. I laugh. "Final bid is nine thousand. And the winner is Miss Maddison Harris!" she says as Enzo smiles and heads over to the woman who won the bid. He high fives all the guys along the way.

"Alright, we are down to the last date to be auctioned off this evening. She's stunning like her mam, the only daughter of Enea and Gráinne—Giovanna! She is currently a student at Crimson working on her medical degree." She smiles as I come out on stage. The crowd cheers and claps. "And go!"

I blush as I hear the bids coming in. As it gets closer to the ten thousand mark, it has come down to four men fighting each other for the win. And it doesn't seem like any of them are going to give up.

"Payback is a bitch isn't it, little brother," my uncle Leo says to my papà, causing him to growl.

Finally, they start to drop off one by one until there is a single bidder left. "Going once, going twice, SOLD! For fifteen thousand to Mr. Declan O'Reilly!"

Declan comes up to the edge of the stage and holds out his hand to me. When I step down, he kisses my cheek and leads me to my family. They've all started to kill Declan with their eyes, which he hasn't noticed yet.

Enea

"Oh fuck no," I swear quietly so only my wife can hear. I start to stand up to go over to Gia.

"Enea...It's for a good cause. Remember that," she says, putting her hand on my chest to calm me down.

I sit back down and glare at Declan. "He needs to stop looking at my baby like she's something to eat," I grumble to Gráinne.

"I know, sweetheart. But she's okay. When it comes to the date, she won't be alone, Grady will be there too."

I can't help but watch Declan as he leans in to talk to my Gia.

"Aren't you going to stop this?" Enzo asks me.

"Yeah this is insane," I hear Bastian say.

The Laurent boys stay quiet. Smart boys.

"I'll deal with the situation in time." My boys stare at Declan. They're quiet now, but I know they won't stay quiet for long.

Chapter Eight

Enea

"Arturo, you're with Grady tonight for Gia. Seamus and Marco, you're with Rella." The girls don't go anywhere without their main guards and tonight are the dates from the charity auction, so I wanted to assign extra help just in case. The auction's such a big deal that you never know what could happen. I know it seems excessive because Rella and Cillian are already a couple. But we've learned to not take chances.

We leave my office and head into the main living area to wait for Declan and Cillian.

Declan

I ring the doorbell and wait. Dom answers the door.

"Right on time." He laughs, stepping back to let me in. "My papà will be here in a few. You're going to have Grady and Arturo with you tonight. Where are you taking Gia?"

"I made reservations at Pierre's." We hear the doorbell and Dom opens the door again to let Cillian in.

As we're waiting for the girls, we see Enea and Leonardo come in with the four guards that'll be with us. It looks like they're coming out of the wall. That's so fucking cool, it's a hidden door behind the staircase. Like their own Bat Cave.

I still don't know why Gia needs guards. I shake Enea's hand. He's a very intimidating man, especially when you're here to take his only daughter out. I shake Leonardo's hand as well.

"Nice to see you, Declan," Enea says in his deep voice.

Yeah, he's scary.

"Nice to see you too, Mr. Mancini," I sputter as he chuckles at me.

"Mr. Mancini's my father. Call me Enea."

Still scary.

There's a rustling noise and we turn towards the staircase to see Gia and Rella standing at the top. I can't stop staring at Gia as she comes down the stairs. I finally get to take her out. When she gets closer, I take her hand and kiss it. She smells so good and holy crap she's stunning. Their mothers follow them down the stairs and go to stand with their fathers.

"You look beautiful," I say to her. She's blushing and oh my god she is the most sublime creature I've ever laid my eyes on. And for tonight, she's mine. Well she's mine forever, she just doesn't know it yet.

We say goodnight to her parents and brothers. I lead her out to my car and open the door for her. I can't stop smiling as I go around the car and get in.

Giovanna

Declan is over the top gorgeous, he's wearing a dark blue plaid suit and his green eyes are shining. For one night he is mine. One look at him and my body feels like it's on fire, like it did the first time I saw him at Dom's game. He's driving one of my favorite cars, an Audi R8. Damn.

"Your car is stunning. I've loved the R8 for years, and you have the manual transmission. That's awesome." His eyes get wide as he looks over at me.

"You know cars?" he asks, pulling out after Cillian.

"I know cars I like." I chuckle. "Not all cars."

"What cars do you like? Do you own any?" He holds my hand in between shifting. I'm trying to concentrate on what he's saying, but the electricity running up my arm every time he touches me is distracting.

"I uh...yeah, sorry. I have a BMW M8 competition coupe and a Ferrari Roma," I finally get out.

"Holy shit! Those are some serious cars. Maybe you can show me next time?"

"Sure! I love driving them. I don't get to as often as I'd like because Grady is usually driving me. But every once in a while I take them out with my brothers. Your suit is really nice." My thoughts are all over the place. He's driving me crazy. But really? Your suit is really nice? What the fuck?

"Have you always liked sports?"

At least he's ignoring my stupid outbursts.

"I've always liked hockey and baseball. Then I started watching MotoGP. I'm also a Leopards, and Stallions fan," I blurt out.

"We should go to games. I can get tickets to any game you would like to go to."

I grin when he says that he can get tickets. Going to a game with Declan would be awesome. GianLuca plays for the Panthers, he's their third baseman. This is his second season and he's doing so well.

"That would be so much fun. Maybe a Panthers game first? My cousin Luca would love it if we went to watch him play."

Declan smiles at me and nods. "It's a date. It's definitely a date."

Declan

I made reservations at Pierre's because I've heard

the food is excellent. They've set up a table for us on the balcony. I'm so nervous, what if she doesn't like it? I requested the private balcony because I wanted her all to myself. Plus this way if there are any fans, they won't be able to come over to us. I love fans, they're a huge part of playing hockey, but tonight I just want to focus on Gia.

She's smiling as I pull up to the restaurant and shake my head at the valet. No one will touch her but me. I hand the valet my keys and go around to help her out of the car. I kiss her cheek and she gives me that smile again. She doesn't know this yet, but I'm hers if she'll have me. If I'm honest, I've been hers since the first time I saw her.

Grady pulls in behind us and gives the valet his keys. He and Arturo are keeping their distance while still staying in view of us.

As we walk through the restaurant, people stare and make comments once they realize who I am. I love that Gia just smiles and keeps walking. It doesn't seem to bother her at all.

When the hostess shows us our seating on the balcony, I watch Gia look out at the view of the city.

"This is spectacular!" Her eyes are sparkling when she looks at me. I can't help but smile back at her.

"Is this okay then?" It's unbelievable how nervous I am. I'm never like this, not even when I'm on the ice. "We can sit in the dining room if you want."

I pull out her chair for her, "No, this is perfect." She smiles.

A waiter comes over carrying an appetizer. "That looks delicious," she says.

"Compliments of Chef Pierre," he tells us when he sets the appetizer down, and I thank him.

I put some of the carpaccio on her plate while she watches me.

"Thank you," she says, taking a bite. She makes a small moaning sound as she closes her eyes, and I have to discreetly adjust myself. Good thing there's a tablecloth to help cover me up. She catches me watching her and covers her face.

She chuckles softly. "Your season has been going really well."

"It's been better since I met you,"

She's shaking her head.

"I doubt that. You've been doing well all season."

"How long have you been a hockey fan?"

"I've been a Redhawks fan since I was about fifteen," she says. "This is going to sound weird but my first live game was the game where I met you."

"Really? Didn't you grow up in Chicago?" I ask her.

"Well, I grew up about three hours west of the city, but we were never able to go to games. I went to Leopards games and Stallions games. But no Redhawks or Panthers. Enzo and I were the only hockey and baseball fans in the house," she says as I give her a puzzled look.

"But Dom's a hockey player." I sound really confused because I am. I'm sure my face matches my tone.

She turns bright red and looks down. "Oh. Well, that's a long story. I didn't grow up with Dom and Bastian."

I try not to push her for more information.

"I hope you'll feel like you can tell me what happened, if not today, maybe one day." I kiss her hand.

"Maybe," she says softly.

What the hell could have happened to my sweet Gia? She didn't grow up with her brothers? And why does she have a bodyguard? I still haven't asked her about that. He's a little intimidating and always on the lookout for something. He makes me a little nervous, like I should be more vigilant about what's going on around us.

Again, I wonder what happened to my girl that she needs to be watched over so much. Could the rumors of the Mancinis being in the mafia be true? Or maybe the family is being targeted because of their wealth?

"That smells amazing!" she exclaims as the main course comes out.

"It does." I chuckle and take a bite of mine. I love steak. Gia ordered the seared salmon. I cut a piece of steak, and she lets me feed it to her.

"Oh my god that's so good!" She cuts a piece of her salmon and feeds it to me.

I smile, then take the bite. "Damn that's a good piece of salmon. It just melts in your mouth—and that sauce!"

"See? I told you fish could be just as good as steak," she teases, making me laugh.

"Well I wouldn't go that far. I mean my steak is really good." She makes a face at me.

"Yeah, yeah, yeah. So what do you like to do when you aren't playing hockey?"

"I love to travel. There are a few things I can't do because of my contract. But I try to have as much fun as I can, especially in the off season. What do you like to do? Did you always want to be a doctor?"

She nods. "I've always wanted to help people, so becoming a doctor seemed like the best way to do that. I considered going into law like Enzo, but I'm not sure this world could handle us both being lawyers." She laughs. "As for free time? I love winter sports, and riding motorcycles and dirt bikes. I love to travel as well. I've been to a few countries, but I want to see more. I like how each country is so different."

"That is so awesome. After seeing you handle the situation with Coach Louis, I think you're going to be a great doctor." I slide my chair closer to her. I can't wait anymore, I need to know if that feeling I had with our first kiss was real. I lean in and kiss her. I hear her make a soft noise as she kisses me back. It was definitely real, and I don't want to kiss anyone else ever again.

"When do you go back to school?" I don't like the idea that Gia will be leaving again. Crimson is a sixteen hour drive or a two and a half hour flight. The plane isn't so bad, but...I want her here with me.

"Lorenzo and I were granted permission to do the rest of the semester remotely. We're not sure if we'll go back to Crimson next fall or transfer to one of the universities here in Chicago," she explains.

I'm so relieved that she's not leaving for now. It will be even better if she transfers to a university here. That way I could see her whenever I want. I watch Gia as she eats the rest of her dinner. She seems to be thinking about a lot of things. I want to ask her what's wrong, but I don't want to scare her away. I'm certain that she is the one I want in my life. I've never wanted anyone like I want her and it's not just sexual. I love how smart she is, how confident she is, yet she also seems so fragile in her own way. I want to hold her and never let anyone hurt her ever again.

"Are you ok, Gia?" I finally ask because she looks so sad. "Is something wrong with the food?"

"No, the food is perfect. This night is perfect," she says as she looks at me.

I wish she would open up to me. Okay, I'm going to do it and just ask why she has bodyguards. I need to know.

"I hope I am not overstepping, but why do you have Grady with you all the time?" I ask her as she chews slowly.

"There are people that don't like my family and Grady is here in case anything were to happen." It feels like she's still avoiding the real reason.

"Should I be worried? Are you in danger?" I frown slightly. "I would never let anyone hurt you." I hold her hand while she talks.

"I know you wouldn't. But you just never know what could happen."

"Can I also ask why you didn't grow up with Bastian and Dom? I know the night we met, I was surprised that Dom had a sister and another brother. We've been teammates for three years and he's never mentioned having twin siblings." She looks a little panicked as she takes a deep breath.

Giovanna

Dammit. I knew he would want to know about Grady and why he has to be with me all the time. And my dumb ass saying that I didn't grow up with Bastian and Dom. I want to tell him about the kidnapping, but I don't fully understand it myself. Since I haven't talked to Dorian, all I know is what Chris told us at dinner. If it was because of the war, I want to hear it from Dorian. I guess I can tell him what I know. If he decides he doesn't want to see me anymore...well what can I really do?

I sigh softly. "Enzo and I were kidnapped when we were two years old. We were raised by another family. About a month before I met you, we found the Mancinis and learned what happened," I blurt out, looking down at my hands. I'm afraid that if I look up, he'll be looking at me like I'm crazy.

He tilts my chin up to look at him.

"How did you find out? And why were you kidnapped?" he asks. I don't see any disbelief in his eyes. He seems sad for me.

"It was right after Christmas break, we were back in Cambridge for school. I wanted to go shopping, so we went to the mall. While we were walking around, I noticed we were being followed by two guys. That's how we met Sebastiano and Domenico. After that, my papà came down, then Dorian showed up—the man we grew up with—and he admitted to kidnapping us. Dorian was a really good dad and he never treated us badly...so it's been really hard." I watch his expressions.

"I'm so sorry that happened to you, Gia," he says softly, while taking my hand. "Thank you for telling me. Is there anything I can do?"

"Thank you. I don't think there is anything anyone can do to help me. I just need to work through it. I have a lot of weird new fears now."

"I want to be here for you," he says as I look down.

"I'm not sure you'll like what you see. I used to feel so secure in everything, but now I'm second guessing a lot." I frown a little. "That's part of the reason Grady goes with me everywhere. My papà doesn't want to take any chances that something could happen again." I take another deep breath. "Enough about me, tell me about you, about this situation with Josie..." I start to ask as he stares at me. "Why do you keep saying the baby isn't yours? I mean are you really sure that you're not the father?"

Declan

I exhale slowly when she asks me about my past and Josie. I don't usually tell anyone about my past. But I'll tell her anything she wants to know.

"My parents died when I was sixteen. It was their twentieth anniversary and they were struck by a drunk driver. My dad died on impact, but my mom held on for a little over a week. I had to tell her we lost my dad, and I believe she died of a broken heart. She and my dad loved each other so much." I go on to tell her about how Henry and Carissa raised me, along with their four children.

"I'm so sorry, Declan. I can't imagine losing both my parents."

"I think that's why I stayed with Josie longer than I should have. I don't like being alone. But I know for certain that the baby isn't mine. The last time I was with Josie was over a year ago."

"Why did you finally break up with her?" she asks me softly.

I can see in her eyes. She's worried that if she's with me, I could leave her and go back to Josie. "I found out she slept with a player on another team. He felt so guilty, he called me to tell me about it the next day," I say as her eyes widen. "But like I said, I knew I wanted out at least a year before that."

"Holy...I'm sorry, Declan," she says as she touches my hand.

"She said I made her feel neglected and that's why she did it. I was relieved. I mean, yes it hurt because she cheated. But I was relieved because it was finally over. I knew in my heart she wasn't the one for me."

"Why didn't you just leave her earlier if you didn't want to be with her?"

"I was scared, and I guess with all the traveling for games, I just kept putting it off. I know it was probably a cop out. In hindsight, I wish I'd just ended it when I first started having doubts about the relationship." I look down at my hands. "Henry and Carissa—they didn't like her from the start. But they didn't say anything until we broke up."

"I understand. It's not easy to end things even when you know it's the right thing to do."

I lean into her and kiss her. Holy shit I'm in heaven. Her lips are so soft and that small moan she lets out as I deepen the kiss is just perfect.

I wrap my arms around her. "You fit perfectly in my arms. You're my penguin." She's everything I've wanted and more. I'm not going to let her get away from me. I thought I knew what love was before, but I was wrong. This is what love really feels like. This is what my parents had and what I've dreamed of having.

"Your penguin? Why, because they mate for life?" She smiles.

"Yes. You're my forever," I whisper.

Chapter Nine

Declan

Last night was the best night ever. Gia's more beautiful inside and out than I ever thought possible. I mean, I already knew she was perfect. But her smile, her laugh, the way she blushes—just takes my breath away. I want to protect her from anything and everything. I hate that she had to go through the trauma of finding out she was kidnapped, I can't even imagine waking up one day and finding out everything you thought was real, wasn't. She's stronger than she thinks, and I'm going to help her through this. I don't know how, but I'll be here for her.

This morning I got a call from Josie. I was so happy from my date with my baby last night, that I didn't even the caller ID before I answered my phone.

She said she wanted to let me know that she had miscarried the baby. I told her I was sorry to hear that. I don't think she was ever pregnant and at this point she had to do something because how would she explain not 'looking' pregnant?

It's such a relief to know it's over and we won't have to deal with her anymore. I can't wait to tell Gia.

Declan: Morning, my beauty

Giovanna: Morning, handsome. Thank you again for last night. I had a really great time. I'm sorry I dumped all that on you. And thank you for telling me about your parents

Declan: Don't be sorry. I'm really glad you told me about it. And I meant it when I said I'll be here for you

Giovanna: I'm here for you too

It makes me sad that she thinks it's a burden to know what she's gone through. Who the fuck kidnaps babies? That's bullshit. I mean, I know there has to be more to it, but still.

I'm glad I told her about my parents, I just wish they were still here to meet her. I miss them so much. But I can't wait to introduce her to my family. They're going to love her.

Giovanna: I'm so happy I met you. What are you doing today?

> Declan: Well, at some point I should
> get out of bed and get my workout in.
> Want to join me?

Giovanna

I smile as I see Declan's text. I really enjoyed being with him last night. He was so sweet and just listened as I told him what I could about the kidnapping—and he didn't push. I think that's why I felt like I could open up to him. He was so patient when I sat there like an idiot trying to decide what to do. But in the end, I feel better that I was able to tell him. I hope it will help him to understand me if we decide to go forward with this relationship. Because I really do want to see where this leads. He makes me feel safe. Even with my insecurities, maybe he could love me for me.

He trusted me enough to tell me about his parents. I could see how much he loves them and misses them. I wish I could've met them. I bet wherever they are, they're so proud of him.

> Giovanna: Sure, where do you
> work out?

> Declan: Actually I have a gym at home
> so I do my warmup and parts of my
> workout here. Then I have practice at
> the rink next to the United Center.
> Afterwards I train with our team trainer

Giovanna: So I'm coming to your place? I mean I can meet you at the rink instead

Declan: Yes, you should come here and then I can drive us to the rink after we're done

Giovanna: Okay, you know that I'll have Grady with me, right?

Declan: Yup! I'm okay with that. In fact, if he wants to, he can work out with us. Do you think your brothers want to come too?

Giovanna: They might, I'll ask them

I text my brothers to see if they want to join Declan and me. Of course they all say yes.

Giovanna: They said they would love to. Dom says he knows where you live and we will be there in about thirty minutes

---

Declan

I can't stop smiling as I read Gia's text. I knew asking if her brothers wanted to work out with us would get her here. I even invited Cillian and Rella. I can't wait to see her.

Declan: That's perfect. I can't wait to
see you. Also, I invited Cillian and Rella

Giovanna: Awesome! See you soon

I look around making sure everything's clean and nothing's thrown about. Living alone makes me a little messy at times. Gia is the first woman I've invited to this house. When I was with Josie, I was renting a condo. After we broke up, I decided to buy a house.

Dom, Cillian, and I work out here together quite often. They have their own gym at home, but they still come here. I don't mind, it's better working out with partners than alone.

I hear a buzz from the gate and I look at the monitor to see Grady in the drivers seat, with another car behind them that I'm assuming is Cillian, Rella, and Marco, Rellas guard. I buzz the gate open and go to the front door to wait for them. I see my Gia getting out. I say hi to all of them as I head straight for Gia and embrace her. I kiss her, causing her to blush and smile.

"My penguin," I whisper. I hear someone clear their throat, making me chuckle.

"Okay, hands off my sister," Enzo says as he shakes his head, making faces at us.

"Yeah, no more of that is needed," Bastian says as he follows Dom to my gym. "You remember Sal and Luca? They wanted to come too, I hope that's okay."

"Of course." I shake Sal and Luca's hands.

"Whoa! You weren't joking when you said full

gym," Enzo says, looking around. "Okay, where can we change?"

"There's a changing area right through there." I point to the door on the left.

"And us? Cause I'm not changing with them," Rella says, pointing at the guys.

I laugh at the look of horror on Rella's face. "You can both change in my room."

"Uh. Your room?" Gia asks, looking around. "We really only need like, a bathroom, maybe?"

She sounds nervous about using my bedroom to change. I'll admit I want her in my bedroom but for reasons that have nothing to do with getting workout clothes on.

"Come on." I chuckle. "It will be easier for you two to use it," I say just as my dog comes barreling in from outside and heads straight for Gia.

"OH MY GOD YOU'RE SO FLUFFY! What's his name?" She's laying flat on her back trying to hug him, but she's laughing too much.

I grab Atlas as I laugh. "This is Atlas. Apparently he likes you."

"He's adorable!" She kisses his face.

Okay, is it normal to be jealous of your own dog? Cause I am. Damn dog. I watch as Atlas greets everyone. He then goes right back to Gia and sits at her feet.

"Okay, time to change," Enzo says after he gets his hugs in with Atlas too.

I take Gia and Rella up to my room. Atlas follows Gia.

"Nice room," Rella says with a smile. "We'll be down in a few."

Gia smiles and heads into my bathroom with Atlas right on her heels.

Rella whispers, "I heard your date went well."

"It was the best night ever," I say as I smile. "I can't wait till our next date."

She grins as she closes the door on me. I head back down to my gym.

Giovanna

How is it Declan gets sexier every time I see him? And Atlas? Oh god, that dog is the cutest thing ever! I look around his bathroom. He's pretty neat, everything seems to have it's place in here. That shower has more heads than I think anyone would need. But I bet they all feel really good when positioned just right—bad Gia. I need to stop imagining being in that damn shower with Declan...I look down and see Atlas giving me a doggie smile. I kneel down and hug him.

After I finish changing, I go back into the bedroom and see Rella waiting.

"Ready?" She smiles.

"Why are you smiling at me like that?" I squint my eyes at her.

"No reason. I just think you and Declan are adorable. He really likes you."

"That's because he doesn't know how crazy I am." I snicker as we head down to the gym.

We see Declan coming up the stairs. He stops us at the top.

"I need to talk to you for a minute," he says.

"We'll meet you in the gym," I say to Rella. She nods and heads downstairs. "Is everything okay?"

My stomach clenches as I look at him. He kisses me, then leads me back to his bedroom and closes the door. I walk over and sit on his bed. Atlas sits next to me like a guard. Declan comes over and sits on the other side of me.

"Everything is fine, baby. In fact it's more than fine." He gets this huge grin on his face.

I love his face and that beautiful smile, but right now it's not making me feel better. I frown as I wait for him to keep talking.

"I talked to Josie this morning."

At the mention of her name I immediately feel my body tense up. Is this where he tells me it's over and that he's decided she's the one for him? I'm pretty sure Atlas can feel the tension because he moves closer to me. It looks like he's glaring at Declan and a low growl is coming out of him.

Declan takes my hand in his, lifts it to his lips and kisses it, then me again.

"Okay. Is this where you tell me that you've

decided to make it work with her?" I barely get it out as I feel that sick feeling again.

He's staring at me like I slapped him and slowly shakes his head.

"There's nothing in this world that could make me leave you, Gia." He keeps his eyes locked on mine. "She called to tell me she miscarried."

I sit there in shock for a minute. Miscarried. I blink a few times and then look into his eyes and see him smiling.

"S-she miscarried?" I stutter out in barely a whisper.

"I don't think she was telling the truth about being pregnant anyway. But it's over, we don't have to deal with her anymore."

I'm still trying to process what he's saying.

"Wow," is all I can say as I sit there. Atlas jumps onto the bed and shoves his wet nose into my neck which makes me giggle. I look at Declan and see him smiling again.

"It's just you and me, baby."

"And Atlas." I chuckle as Declan makes a face at Atlas.

He leans over and kisses me as Atlas growls at him.

"She was mine first," he says to Atlas, who barks back at him.

"I think he just said no." I burst out laughing. I hug Declan. "I'm sorry if she really was pregnant and she miscarried. But I'm also relieved that it's over."

"Me too, baby. Me too."

We spend the next two hours working out in different pairs, including a little sparring between me and my brothers. It's been a really good day.

"So now you three head to the United Center to practice?" I ask as we all relax a bit.

"Yeah, you and Rella can come and watch if you want," Cillian says with a nod.

"How much time do we have?" Rella asks, looking at Cillian.

"We should leave in about forty-five minutes," he says as the others head to the showers. No one wants to get into the cars all sweaty and icky.

"Um, can we use your shower?" I ask Declan.

"Of course. I'll get you a couple of towels, you can use this shower if you want Rella," he says as he stops in front of what looks like a guest bathroom.

Fiorella grabs one of the towels from him. "Thanks!"

I follow him back to his room and he closes the door behind us. He backs me up against the wall and kisses me until I'm out of breath. I run my hands down his back.

"Fuck, Declan," I whisper as I look into his green eyes.

"God I love you, you're so fucking sexy," he says, panting slightly.

I moan as I feel his length pressing into my abdomen. I grab his ass and I kiss him roughly. I gasp when I feel his hands slide under my shirt. I bite his lip, he growls and grinds into me more.

"Fuck, I want you so damn bad," he pants, lifting me up and heading to the bathroom. As he sets me down, I look at him.

I put my hand on his chest as I catch my breath. "I want you too Declan, but I just can't yet."

He puts his forehead on mine and takes a few deep breaths, then kisses me softly.

"I'll wait as long as you need, Gia." He adjusts himself. "Go shower and then we can leave. I do want you to ride with me."

I smile and nod at him. "I'd like that. Grady can ride with my brothers. They won't like it, but too bad." I kiss him. "I'll be out in a minute."

Holy shit that was fucking crazy. I almost had sex with Declan with my brothers downstairs. What the fuck is wrong with me? He drives me insane. And then it finally hits me. Did he say he loved me? There's no way. I must've heard him wrong.

I quickly shower, dry off and get dressed. I laugh at myself in the mirror. I must be hallucinating to think he said he loved me. I hear Rella calling my name as she comes into the room.

"Are you ready?" she asks as I come out.

"I'm ready." I grab my stuff and follow her out.

"Okay, we should get to the rink," Dom says, we all nod and start to head outside.

"I'm going to ride with Declan," I say to Grady, causing him to frown. "Stop that. We're all going to the same place and you can ride with the others."

"You know the rules, Gia," he says quietly.

"I should be able to ride with Declan. You followed us in a separate car when we went on our date, and it was fine. I would like to spend some time with him alone," I explain and he finally nods.

"Fine. I know you want some time. But if anything happens, you'll have to answer to your papà."

"I know. I really do understand." I kiss his cheek. Then I get in the car with Declan and lean over to kiss him.

"I don't know if you heard me earlier. I love you, Gia. I never believed in falling in love so fast. But you're everything I've ever dreamed of. It's okay if you can't say it yet. I just want you to know how I feel."

Holy shit he did say it on purpose, and now he said it again. I look into his eyes. "I've never felt this way about anyone either, I just need to get my shit together and I don't want to hurt you in the process." The truth is, I do love him. I'm just too much of a chicken to say it. Bwak bwak bwak.

"The only way you could hurt me is if you leave me. I can deal with anything else."

I kiss him again as Dom honks behind us. We laugh when we hear him yell at us to move.

Chapter Ten

Declan

We didn't make the playoffs this year. It was a hard season, and we had a lot of key guys out with injuries. But at least now we can all heal up and come back stronger next season.

Since we're not playing in the finals, I have the summer off. I need to be back in August for training camp, but I have the next three months to spend with my Gia. I'm beyond excited to get to know her better and to help her see how we're meant to be forever. I know she has her insecurities and I understand all of them. She worries when the puck bunnies come onto me, it's just going to take some time for her to see it doesn't mean anything. Hell I don't like it when I see guys flirting with her either. And that happens a lot.

We already have a trip planned with her whole family. We're going to Italy to see her uncle Aiden's MotoGP race. I'm really excited to go to my first live race—I watch them on TV but I've never been able to go to a live one. I've also never been to Italy, so to be able to experience both things with my girl is the best.

Gia's still dealing with the aftermath of learning about her past, but she's working through it. She talks to me about it and I can see that she is doing a lot better now than a few months ago. She's a strong, magnificent spitfire that I'll never walk away from.

I've also changed how I deal with fans. I realized that I can't let them cross lines that I wouldn't want Gia crossing.

I plan on asking her to move in with me. I would've done it already, but I don't think her dad would be okay with that. I also think that if she says yes, Grady will be coming too. It's a good thing that I have lots of space here. And rooms on the opposite side of my house for Grady.

Giovanna

I'm on my way to Declan's house with my brothers, cousins, and of course Grady, so that we can all work out together. I love seeing my Declan every day. We make sure we take time to be together no matter what we have going on. Working out is just the start of our day, after that we sometimes go to the rink and skate for fun or just stay at his house and hang out. It's been a great few months so far, and at this point, I can't imagine my life without him in it.

I head inside when we get to Declan's and see Atlas. I love that dog so much. Whenever I'm here, he's glued to my side.

"Hi, baby!" I laugh as Atlas knocks me down and slobbers all over my face. I hear a low chuckle and look up to see the most handsome face.

"Hi, my love." Declan laughs as he pries Atlas off me, then helps me up and gives me the biggest hug. I love being in his arms, he makes me feel safe, like nothing could ever hurt me.

"Ahem." We hear Bastian.

I squint my eyes at him.

"Yes, Bastian? Maybe you should go work out and stop watching us, you creeper."

Rella snorts.

My brothers laugh as they head into the gym. I grumble under my breath about how they're a pain in my ass. Declan snickers as he holds me.

"So not funny. It'll be nice when they go home." I kiss him and then head up to his room with Rella to change.

We pair up and do our workouts as usual, then we get in the pool to cool off. Even though it's the off season for the hockey guys, they still have to keep in shape.

When we're at the arena, Rella and I skate and the

boys play their own version of a scrimmage. If their teammates are in town, they come down and join in.

Grady and Marco have been working out with us too. Lately, I've started to see Grady as more of a family member than my guard. He told me that he wishes he had been around when Enzo and I were taken because he would've killed whoever touched us. But that happened before Grady's time. He's been with the Mancini family for about ten years now.

My brothers and cousins have finally left and it's just the two of us. Well okay, three. But Grady has gone to his room. Declan set it up for the nights I stay over.

Declan

I sit at the island in the kitchen and watch Gia make sandwiches for us. I love how she looks in my house. This is where she belongs. Atlas is where he always is, right at her feet. I think that damn dog thinks she's his now. I growl at Atlas when he looks at me and I swear that dog rolls his eyes, then looks back at Gia and licks her leg. I hear her giggle and I sigh. That's the best sound in the world.

"Move in with me," I say to her, causing her to turn around slowly, her eyes wide.

"What did you say?"

"Move in with me, Gia. I want us to be like this every day. I want to go to bed and wake up with you every day. I hate it when you leave. I want to go to my away games and come home to you," I blurt out.

"Y-you want me to live with you?"

"Yes. I knew you were the one for me the day I met you. You're everything to me and I don't think we should wait." I get up and wrap my arms around her, I can see the worry in her eyes.

Atlas grumbles at me as he tries to wriggle between us.

"I want you forever, Gia. If I thought your papà would say yes, I would marry you right now."

Grady appears in the kitchen as I finish my speech, shaking his head.

"You know Enea won't give you his blessing right now." He grabs a couple of sandwiches and looks at the two of us. He then turns, makes himself a drink, and goes back to his room. Creeper.

I hear Gia giggle as we watch him.

"Why are you laughing?"

"Because he pops up like a jack-in-the-box and then disappears back into his room."

I kiss her. "So what do you think? Move in with me?"

"You know I can't, Declan. I'm not saying not ever, just not now. My papà won't be okay with it. I know I'm an adult, but after everything that's happened, I just can't leave my parents yet."

"I know, but I want you here with me." I sound like I'm whining, but I don't care. I desperate to have her here with me. I'll keep working on her while we are in

Italy. We leave in a week and I'm super excited because it's our first vacation together. We're planning on staying for two weeks, maybe three. We agreed to leave it open and figure it out when we get there.

Giovanna

I want to live with Declan. But I need to get my shit together before I do. I need to deal with the kidnapping and with Dorian. I don't know if I'm ready or strong enough to hear what he has to say yet. I wasn't lying when I said my papà won't be okay with it. But there'll be a time when he'll have to be, because Declan is my future.

Declan has done so much to help me figure all of this out. Besides finding my real family, finding Declan has been the best thing to happen to me.

He told me the other day that being with me has helped him miss his parents a little less. That I've filled the void in his soul that he's carried around with him since that night. And the sadness that I've been carrying around since the day at the mall feels like it's finally starting to fade. Declan is the reason for that.

I'm excited to go on our first vacation together. My papà and brothers haven't stopped giving him death stares yet, but they'll come around. Dom is the only one on Declan's side, and that's probably because they're teammates.

Chapter Eleven

Giovanna

I stretch as I hear the stewardess say that we're starting to make our descent into Bologna, Italy. I smile at Declan and give him a kiss.

"Hi, beautiful. I love you."

"Are you ready to see some racing?" I still haven't told him I love him. Even though I do, I just haven't said it yet.

"I can't wait." He smiles. The plane touches down and we wait for the 'fasten seat belt' lights to turn off so we can get our carry-ons down.

"Thank you," I say to Declan as he hands my bag to me. I laugh when he won't let go of it.

"You know I can carry my own bag." I poke him in

the chest. I see an older couple smiling at us. I smile back at them as we wait to get off the plane.

Grady is chuckling at us. He's gotten used to our banter by now.

As we deplane, I see the stewardess wink and slip Declan something. He reaches into his pocket and pulls it out. Without even looking at the paper, he hands it back to her. She frowns at him and tries to hand it back to him.

I love being with Declan, but I'm still having problems with all the women who continuously throw themselves at him. Like this stewardess, it doesn't matter to them if I'm here or not. I know he wants me and would never cheat on me, but it still bothers me.

"Thank you, but no thank you," he says to her, taking my hand and walking off the plane.

We make our way to the baggage claim and wait for our suitcases to come out. I'm still smiling because of the look on the stewardess's face when he gave her the piece of paper back. I feel his arms around me and lean into him.

"Thank you," I whisper.

"For what, baby?"

"For not taking her number. She was gorgeous."

"Sure, she was pretty. But I'm in love with the most gorgeous woman ever." He kisses me.

How did I get so lucky?

"She tried to give me her number after you gave it back to her." Grady snorts.

"What did you do?" I ask.

"I told her no thanks." Grady smiles.

While we wait for our luggage to come down the chute, I call the number for the car that's picking us up.

"The car will be here in fifteen minutes," I tell Declan and Grady as I hang up.

We finally see our bags and grab them, then make our way to the designated pickup location.

The driver pulls up in front of the hotel beside the valet stand. The valet opens my door and smiles at me while extending his hand to help me out.

"Grazie."

We're staying at one of the most beautiful hotels in Bologna. There are huge stone columns at the front and stained glass windows wrapping around the ground floor. It's magnificent. My parents told me they always stay here when they visit.

"You're welcome. Enjoy your stay." The valet continues to smile at me.

I hear Declan quietly making rude comments as we walk into the lobby. I chuckle, taking his hand.

"Hi, reservations for Mancini," I say to the concierge.

He smiles. "Penthouse 7 for three weeks. You're

the last Mancini to check in." Declan clears his throat as he stands with his hand on my back.

"H-here are your keys. Did you need more than two?" he asks, looking at Declan then me.

"Could we get three keys?" I ask.

"Yes, just give me a minute to code another one."

"Thank you."

I take the keys while Declan gathers our luggage.

"Elevators are to your left," the concierge says.

"Grazie."

Grady is sharing a room with Marco, which is on the same floor as ours.

"I'll see you at dinner, let me know if you two decide to go out before then," he says to us.

"Okay, you're next door to us, right?"

"Yeah. Marco will be here in a minute, we're gonna take a quick look around."

"Don't you want to take your bags up first?" I ask.

"Nah, I want to look around first."

"Okay, see you at dinner." I hand him one of our room keys and then wave bye to him.

"Do you want me to carry something?" I ask Declan while we wait for the elevator. He seems annoyed.

We get into the elevator and I open my mouth to ask him if he is okay. He pins me against the wall and kisses me roughly.

"You are mine and I am yours. There is no one else," he growls.

Right as I'm about to answer him, the elevator

comes to a stop. A family steps in and chooses their floor. I smile at the little girl staring at me and she smiles back as they get off at their floor.

He kisses me again, though softer than before. "I'm sorry, baby. I fucking hate watching men flirt with you." The elevator opens on our floor.

I step out and follow Declan to the penthouse doors that lead to our suite.

I step inside after him, close and lock the door, then grab the back of his shirt and turn him to face me. I kiss him roughly, letting out a moan.

"There will never be anyone but you," I whisper.

"Te amo. You are my love, my heart," he says softly, looking down at me. "You're the only one I'll ever want."

I let Declan lead me into the bedroom and lay me down, running his hands under my shirt and kissing me. So far we haven't had sex, and trust me when I say it has been really hard not to rip his clothes off every day. I know Declan has had his share of women. Me? I've only been with one person. That's part of my insecurity. What if I'm not good at it?

I reach for his belt, unbuckle it, then pull the buttons on his jeans open.

"Are you sure?" he asks, his voice low and breathy.

I nod as he takes my shirt off. I help him get my bra off. He licks his lips as he watches me.

"God, you are more beautiful than I imagined," he whispers. He slowly licks and sucks each of my nipples while I whimper his name. I help him get my jeans off.

I hear his breathing get faster as he yanks his off. I nibble down his chest, making my way down to his beautiful cock. I lick the precum off the tip and hear him inhale sharply. I slowly wrap my lips around him. I will never get all of him in my mouth. He's way too big, but I'll do my best. I start to move my mouth up and down, using my hands for the shaft, causing Declan to moan louder.

"Oh god, Gia. Fuck yes," he gasps, running his hands through my hair.

I frown when he pulls me off him.

"I want to be inside you when I come," he says, kissing me. Then he makes his way down my body to my clit.

"Declan." I feel him slide a finger into me while he licks and sucks. "Please, Declan. I need to feel you." I gasp when I feel him kiss his way back up my body as he keeps pumping his finger in me, then slides another in. "Fuck!" I grip the bed sheet. "Baby, please," I beg.

I hear him open the condom wrapper. I open my eyes and watch him put it on.

"Are you ready?" He rubs himself on my slit as I nod. I feel him slowly push into me. "Look at me Giovanna," he whispers, fighting to keep his voice steady. I open my eyes and look into his as he keeps pushing into me.

"Fuck, you are so damn tight, my love." He slows down. "Everything about you is perfect. Are you okay?" he asks as he stops moving, letting me get used to his size.

I kiss him and grab his ass, making him move. He watches me as he pulls out a little and pushes back in.

"Sì, amore mio," I murmur softly as he starts to move faster.

"I'm not going to be able to last long, baby. I'm sorry," he moans.

I feel him rub my clit as I move with him.

"Fuck, yes!" I feel my climax getting closer. "Fuck me, Declan," I growl as I start to see stars. He moves faster, then my orgasm takes over and I gasp his name. I hear him growl mine as he comes right after, pulsing in me while I clench myself on him. I try to steady my breathing while I hold him.

"That...was the best ever," he gets out, holding me tight. "You're mine forever, Giovanna Aoife Mancini."

"And you're mine, Declan Rowan O'Reilly. I love you," I say softly, kissing him. He gives me the biggest smile.

"You love me?" he teases, kissing me again.

"Yes!" I laugh as I hold him.

I hear a text come in and reach for my phone—it's my uncle Aiden in our family chat. I respond to his text while Declan gets up and throws the condom away.

Uncle Aiden: Are we meeting up for dinner?

Enea: Yes. What time and where?

Everyone texts okay.

My uncle Aiden rides for Ducati's factory team. It's

the start of a new season and that's why we've all come to Italy.

Declan and I are the last ones to get here because I had a final to take. He waited to travel with me. We also had Grady with us for protection, as always.

> Uncle Aiden: L'Amore at 7pm.
> Reservations are under O'Connor

Everyone texts okay again.

"We have three hours," I say to Declan. I lay my head on his chest and yawn.

I hear a rumble in his chest as he chuckles. "Maybe a nap?" he says softly.

"My penguin," I murmur as I doze off, snuggled in his arms.

We meet in the lobby to wait for the cars that will take us to the restaurant. I lean my head on Declan's chest, listening to everyone around us talk.

"Amore mio. *Il mio pinguino*," I hear him whisper. My love. My penguin.

I smile as I hold him. Rella comes over with Cillian and takes a selfie of the four of us and posts it on her Instapost page.

Instapost

> Fiorella: Dinner with some of my
> favorite people #CillianAndFiorella
> #DeclanAndGiovanna #Family
> #Famiglia

She also tags the three of us in the pic. I 'like' the pic and leave a message.

> Giovanna: Perfect night with the best
> people (heart emoji)

> Declan: My baby is sexy (heart eyes
> emoji) RAWR #MyPenguin (penguin
> emoji)

> Domenico: EW. NO. HANDS OFF MY
> SISTER, DECLAN! (knife emoji)
> #BadDeclan #HandsOff #MySister

> Cillian: My world. My family. Always
> (heart emoji)

> Lorenzo: I have the best twin
> #ManciniTwins #LorenzoAndGiovanna
> #BackOffDeclan (knife emoji)

He tags Declan and me as he laughs.

> Giovanna: My twin is the best. (heart
> emoji) Love you so much, Enzo

> Declan: Make me. (fist emoji) She's
> mine now (smiley devil emoji)
> #IlMioMondo #IlMioPinguino (penguin
> emoji)

We laugh as we get into the cars and head to the restaurant.

Fifteen minutes later we arrive at the restaurant. When we get out, my mam sees my uncle Aiden and rushes to hug him.

"Hi, big brother," she smiles, kissing his cheek.

He smiles as he hugs her tight. "Hi, sis. You look beautiful," he says in his thick Irish accent, then hugs everyone else. I introduce Declan to my uncle. He's being nice, but I can see him watching Declan closely.

"Hello," he says to the hostess. "We're all here now." She nods and blushes as she looks at all of us.

"R-right this way." She stares at Declan, then leads our group to the private room we've reserved. She stands to the side of the door to let us through. Declan and I are some of the last to go in. "You're Declan O'Reilly, defenseman for the Chicago Redhawks, and you're Cillian McGregor!" she exclaims.

Declan and Cillian both nod at her.

"I'm from Chicago, you're my favorite players!"

She steps closer to them.

I pull away and try not to frown as I walk to my chair.

"Thank you," they both say, walking past her.

Declan follows me and holds my chair as I sit down.

"It never stops," Rella grumbles while we sit down.

"Even in Italy." I snort. I feel Declan kiss my neck and I shake my head at him, then make a face, which he chuckles at.

"Amore mio," he says softly I turn to look at him.

"It's still weird to see people react to you like that, I'm sorry," I say softly.

"I understand, my love. I know how I feel when men come onto you, it makes me want to rip their arms off. So I get it." He kisses my head.

"I'm going to the bathroom," Rella says, grabbing me to go with her. I give Declan a kiss and follow Rella.

"You okay, Gia?" she asks as she goes into a stall.

"Yeah, I'm okay. I'm still not used to the fans yet. Declan's been so much better at not letting them get too close to us, but sometimes it just happens. It's the ones like her that look at him like she wants to eat him. Those are the worst." I wash my hands. "I want to claw that hostess's eyes out just for looking at him." She chuckles at me. It's funny how possessive I get when women react like that to Declan.

"I know exactly how you feel, Gia. Cillian has women come onto him too. I have to really try not to get angry, but I do. Even after two years, it's still not easy. And I don't think it will ever be," she says.

Knowing that Rella feels the same way as I do makes me feel less crazy. Walking out of the restroom, I glance over at the hostess and she smirks at me. The only thing that stops me from going over and smashing my fist in her face is my papà's voice.

"Mi passerotta, leave it alone. Per favore," he says in my ear.

I take a deep breath and follow my papà and Rella back to the dining room. Declan stands when he sees me. I try to brush past him, but he takes my arm and tells my papà we need to go outside for a minute.

My papà nods and gestures for Grady to go with us. We hear the hostess make a purring noise at Declan as we walk past her.

I slow down and almost come to a stop, but Declan keeps me moving out the door. Grady positions himself so that I can't see the hostess through the glass.

"My love, please," he says, making me look at him.

I don't know why I'm mad at him, I mean it isn't even his fault. "Just let me deal with this."

He gets in my face. "You're everything to me, baby." He wraps his arms around me. I struggle a bit against him. "I'm not going to let you go, so you can stop trying to get away," he says and I finally sigh, melting into his arms as I wrap mine around him.

"I'm sorry," I whisper.

"You have nothing to be sorry for. That girl is an ass. There's always going to be fans like that. They think they can disrespect you. And that I'll cheat with them." He holds me tighter. "But that will never happen."

"I'll try to do better, Declan, I promise. But it's just so frustrating." I feel calmer when he holds me.

"It's really okay, baby. I understand why you feel this way."

I lean up and start to nibble his lower lip as I moan softly. I hear him moan too.

"If you keep doing that, we'll have to go back to the hotel," he whispers.

We hear Grady clear his throat.

I make a face at Grady. We turn and head back into the restaurant.

"Can I talk to you for a minute?" the hostess says to Declan as we walk inside.

"No, sorry. I appreciate you being a fan, but tonight is about our family."

"I just wanted to invite you to a party at Club Mark tonight," she practically shouts at him.

Declan ignores her as we go back to the room.

We see a group of guys being led into the room as we're getting our drinks. My Uncle Aiden smiles, stands, then goes over to them. I recognize them as MotoGP riders. My uncle introduces them and everyone says hi. They sit down to join us for dinner.

"We should all go out after dinner," one of the riders, Marc, suggests.

"Sure, but where is there to go?" Sal asks as we get our appetizers and second round of drinks.

"There's a club about fifteen minutes away. It's a good place to hang out and dance. You can shoot pool too, or just sit and drink," he replies.

"Demonico's?" asks Francesco, another rider, as Marc nods. "That's a good place."

Chapter Twelve

Giovanna

After dinner, our parents head back to the hotel. The rest of us decide to go out with the riders.

We get out of the cars at the club and follow the Moto guys in.

"So what do you do?" Francesco asks me.

"I have two more years until I graduate from medical school," I say in Italian.

"That's awesome! Your Italian is really good."

"Our parents taught us."

"I'm from Turin, in northern Italy."

"I've been to Turin. It's beautiful there. But I love Tuscany."

"Tuscany is beautiful, yes," he says in broken

English. "Maybe I show you Rimini. It is where I train a lot."

"That would be nice. I've been there before. I think Declan would like it there too." I lean on Declan, pulling him into the conversation.

"Would you like to dance?" I hear someone ask me. It's Maverick, another GP rider.

"Sure." I give Declan a kiss before I follow him. When we get to the dance floor, I see Rella dancing with one of the other riders. The music changes to a sensual Latin song. Maverick keeps getting closer to me, but I try to maintain some space between us.

I look over to see Cillian cutting in to dance with Rella. I feel Maverick's hands on my hips as he dances behind me.

"You're so beautiful," Maverick says as we dance.

"Thank you." He tries to grab my hand.

"Take. Your hands. Off. My girl," Declan growls at Maverick.

I turn to Maverick. "Thank you for the dance." He starts to say something, but I let Declan pull me away.

"I told you, Gia. You're mine. No one is allowed to touch you," he says in a low voice.

I don't always feel like I'm his. I know it's my own fucking fault, but it's so hard when there's girls like that hostess. My logical side says of course he would never hurt me or leave me. But then there's the side that goes *what if?* What if he decides I'm not worth the trouble? What if the next girl is better than me? Fuck. I think I just said I don't belong to him. I was thinking it for a second, but I didn't mean to say it out loud. The look on his face tells me that yup, I said it out fucking loud...

Declan

"If you want my sister to be yours, you have to be hers too," I hear Dom say to me. We're watching Gia dance with that damn racer. "Women are always going to come onto us. I know she's dealing with it the best she can, but it's hard for her sometimes."

"Fuck! I know! I tell them 'no' right away. I don't want them touching me or giving me their damn numbers. All I want is Gia." I feel my temper rising fast as I watch her dance with Maverick. I want to snap his arms off—let's see how well he can ride his motorcycle with no fucking arms.

I've reached my limit and go over to break it up. I know she's upset, but I don't care. She's mine and fuck if I will watch another man touch her. I don't care if they're just dancing.

I look at Gia. She just told me she doesn't belong to me. "The hell you don't. You're mine, Gia." I finally feel her relax as she dances with me. "I told you earlier after we made love that you're mine forever."

"Why do you want this? You have all these women that just throw themselves at you. They'd do anything to be with you. Yet you put up with my shit and my stupid insecurities."

I hate that she sounds so damn sad. I know in time she will feel better about it. I won't give up on her. I don't care how many times I have to tell her.

"Baby, you need to listen to me. I love you. I've loved you from the moment I saw you. You're mine, and I will never want anyone but you. I thought I knew what love felt like, but I didn't know anything till I met you. This. This is what love is—you and me." I hold her tight and feel her mold herself to me.

"You and me," I hear her whisper as we dance.

Giovanna

I don't know why Declan puts up with my shit. I still can't seem to get this crap out of my head. I know I love Declan, I wouldn't have said it earlier if I didn't, and I know he loves me. But that hostess just struck a nerve and kicked my stupid fears into overdrive. Fucking Dorian. I was never an insecure person before my world blew up. Now I have trust issues, and when I see women trying to slip him their numbers, or even their underwear—which is disgusting, by the way—I get so angry. Even when he tells them to fuck off, in a nice way of course, I'm still pissed. I know that's how he feels when men hit on me. I love everything about him, I just hope I don't fuck this up. Losing him would be devastating.

After the song ends, we return to our group.

Everyone is ordering more drinks.

"Are you enjoying riding the Ducati?" I ask Francesco, who says to call him Pecco.

"It is very different from Moto2. But a fun challenge. Have you been to a race before?"

"I've been to a lot of races. This will be Declan's first live race, though."

"You have passes to get in the rider area?"

"Yes, my zio Aiden made sure we all got our passes."

"You both have to come see my bike. You can sit on it." He smiles at Declan and me.

"That would be awesome!" Declan says with a huge smile.

Declan

"You ride motorcycles too?" Pecco asks.

"I do, I have two bikes, a *Harley* and a *Ducati*."

"That's awesome! Which *Ducati* do you have?"

"I have the *Panigale V4*, but I don't get to ride it much. I'm not allowed to ride during hockey season."

"How come?"

"It's in my contract."

"But you are okay to ride when you are on vacation?"

"Yes, during summer break I can ride."

Pecco nods at me. "Did you watch racing before

you met Giovanna?"

"I started watching about five years ago. Now I watch it every chance I get, but I've never been to a live race."

Pecco nods. "I understand, I have a hard time following other sports sometimes too. But now I think I would like to watch you play hockey. Our season ends in November, maybe I can come see you play."

"That would be great! We can definitely get you tickets for a game. November is perfect because our season starts in October. Just let us know when you'd like to come. You can meet the team if you want."

"Thank you. I really appreciate that."

MotoGP races are crazy! There's so much going on in the paddock. We got to meet more of the riders there. And Pecco did let Gia and I sit on his bike, it was so fucking cool.

I thought getting ready for a hockey game was a process—these guys have so much more to do. They have two days of practice and then they have qualifying. Finally, on Sunday, they race. The excitement on race day rivals game night for us. The crowds are loud and the bikes are louder. I wish there was a bigger following for this in the United States. I would definitely be at every race I could get to. There used to be three tracks that MotoGP raced at—Laguna Seca in California, Indianapolis Motor Speedway in Indiana, and Circuit of the Americas in Texas. But now they only race in Texas.

Everyone decided to stay in Italy for three weeks. Because of that, we were able to go to another race in Spain, and it was just as spectacular as the one in Italy. Spending these last few weeks with my Gia has been the best time of my life. It's definitely helped us grow closer as a couple.

Giovanna

I know that my issues won't go away on their own, but I've started to realize that Declan really does want to stick around. We talked more about the kidnapping and about how I don't know how to forgive Dorian—I don't want to be mad at him forever. We also talked about how much I miss my Laurent brothers. He suggested that maybe I should talk to Dorian and ask him all the questions that I have. I'm thinking he's right. It might help me to get past the anger.

We also spent time talking about his parents and his childhood. I really wish I could've met his parents. They sound like such a loving couple and they loved Declan so much. He got his middle name from his dad.

On the plane to go home, I lay my head on his shoulder once we get settled in our first-class seats.

"We need to go on more vacations. I want to travel everywhere with you," he says.

"Maybe we can do more traveling next summer? My parents won't want us to travel during winter since this will be our first holiday season as a family."

"That sounds good. Is there anywhere you would like to go?"

I shake my head. "Nowhere specific. Well, maybe Ireland? My mam is from Galway and I would love to see it. My parents may want to come with us if we go there, and I'd like to come back to Italy. Where do you want to go?" I snuggle into him.

"Ireland sounds great, my father's parents were from Cork. I would love to see it. Although anywhere you want to go is fine by me, as long as we can go together."

"I feel the same way. We could just drive across the US and I'd be happy. It would be an adventure for us. Well us and Grady." I snicker.

Grady looks at us from across the aisle and squints his eyes at me.

I remember last year, when all I could think about was finishing med school. Now, all I can think about is spending time with my family and Declan.

"I love you, Gia."

"I love you, Declan."

How did I get so lucky?

Giovanna

With everything that has happened, I'm starting to question if I want to continue my career in medicine. Do I really want to be a surgeon? Maybe I can do something else after I finish med school, bit this is something I'll have to decide in the next year or so. Another factor is that I miss Declan. I can't go to away games because of school and it will only get harder if I continue on this path.

The only thing I'm sure of right now is my decision to transfer to Wildcat. It's too far of a commute for us to live in Lake Renegade Township, so our parents have helped us purchase a house in Evanston. Sebastiano and Domenico live there with us.

Declan and I have been together for a little over six

months, but it feels like years. We still have issues, but who doesn't? Things have been pretty good for the most part. I still have problems with some of the women that come around, but he has been better with being more conscious about how he reacts to them. I know he can't just tell them off because it would be bad for his image.

I've also met Henry, Carissa and their kids. The oldest three are in college and the youngest graduates high school this year. They're so much fun to be around and I can't wait for them to meet my family.

Then there's the Josie situation—we thought she was out of our lives when she said she had miscarried. Now she's claiming Declan came to her the night his hockey season ended. That he was distraught because the team had lost their chance at the playoffs. So once again, she's claiming that he slept with her and she's pregnant. I know that's a lie because he was with me. But like the last time, she's been telling anyone who will listen, including the media, that she's having Declan's baby. So now we have to wait—again—till the baby is born to do a paternity test.

There's one thing I feel bad about. He still doesn't know about my family's 'business'. Not the legitimate business that is Mancini Legacy Enterprises, but the other side that is, and always will be, mafia. I don't know how to bring it up, and as of now I'm still forbidden to say anything about it to him anyway. I'm afraid that when he does find out, he's going to be upset. I mean, he didn't sign up to be with someone like me. I told him about the kidnapping, but not in full detail. Just that it happened. Right now, he thinks my papà is just a businessman and my mam is a housewife.

How do you explain that your papà is the head of the Chicago mafia? And that you were kidnapped by the head of another mafia? Yeah, I don't know either. But if I want to be with him, I need to figure out how to do that. I'll need to talk to my papà first to ask permission. I'm not directly involved with the day to day aspects of what he does, so I'm hoping he'll say yes.

I head downstairs to find my papà and knock on his office door before going in.

"Hi, Papà. Are you busy?" I ask, sitting down on the couch.

"*Mi passerotta.* I always have time for you. What's going on?"

"I wanted to talk to you about Declan."

"What about him?"

"I want to tell him about you. About the family, the real reason that Enzo and I were kidnapped." I see him start to shake his head no. "I love him. I want him to know everything about me." I rush getting it all out before I lose my nerve.

"Baby, I know what you mean. But what if you tell him and it doesn't work out? Do you really think that he's the one? And if he's not, are you sure that he won't say anything to anyone?"

I know in my heart that Declan is the one. He would never betray me or the family. I'm positive about that.

"I trust him. I know that he will understand. You, Zio Leo and Zio Tonio have made sure that just about everything we do is legal now. We own hotels, restaurants, shops, and we just opened Luminescence."

We also back MMA fighters, usually the up-and-coming ones. My papà likes to help them achieve their dreams. He believes everyone needs help at one time or another in their lives.

"But we still make sure this city follows our rules, mi passerotta. There are consequences when those rules are broken."

"I know, Papà. Please let me tell him," I beg.

"Okay, amore. You can tell him. But he needs to understand the importance of keeping what we do in the family. This isn't something to take lightly."

"I'll explain it all, Papà. Thank you." I get up and hug him. I hope that Declan will understand.

I text Declan to see if he is free for dinner.

Giovanna: Hi, amore. Are you free to have dinner with me tonight?

Declan: I always have time for you. Practice will be over at four, pick you up at six? Where do you want to go?

Giovanna: Maybe we can just go to our favorite beach spot and have a picnic? I can make us some sandwiches

Declan: That sounds perfect, amore. I'll see you at six. I love you

> Giovanna: I love you too. Have a good
> practice

I sit and fidget while I wait for Declan to show up. It feels like time is crawling on purpose. It's doing it to torture me, I just know it. When I finally hear his car outside, I jump up to quickly grab the blanket and picnic basket I put together.

I run past my mam and Bastian. "Bye love you!" I open the front door and bounce off of Declan. "Shit."

"I missed you too." He catches me, chuckles, then gives me a kiss. As we're walking to his truck, he takes the blanket and basket from me. He puts them in the back seat, then goes around to get in, leaning over to kiss me again. "My love."

When we get to our favorite spot, we spread the blanket out and set the picnic basket on it. I sit down and let out a small sigh.

"What's wrong, Gia? The look on your face is worrying me."

"I need to tell you something, and it's a really big something. But I don't want this to change things. Or scare you away." I play with my hands while I talk.

"Baby, we've been through this. There's nothing that could ever make me leave you."

I take a deep breath. "Okay, so you know how my papà is a businessman, right? Well there's more to it. Have you heard of the Chicago mafia?"

"I've heard rumors. Everyone has, right? I mean, it's Chicago. Wait, is that what you were talking about with you and Enzo being kidnapped?" he blurts out.

"My papà is the head of the Chicago mafia. Dorian Laurent is the head of the Springfield mafia. Our families have been at war for the last 100 years and it started back in Europe. But my papà has worked really hard with my uncles to make the organization a legitimate business. In the old days, they ran guns and drugs. But never trafficking. Dorian claims he saved us —that Enzo and I were alone and crying, so he rescued us. But my papà says that's impossible. None of us were ever left alone because of what was going on at the time."

"So wait. Dorian stole you and Enzo to hurt your family? Because your papà is the head of the Chicago Mafia?"

"That's what we think. Until I talk to Dorian, I won't know his side. I don't even know if what he says will really matter. The bottom line is, he kidnapped us."

"What does that mean for you? When it comes to you being a doctor, I mean. What will your role in the family be then?"

"I would only help when needed. I'd probably do my residency at Lucciola Memorial..." I trail off because I know that my father is still a very powerful man in our city. People know his name and either respect or fear it.

It feels like Declan's pulling back a little. I don't know what to say.

I silently hand him a sandwich and a water bottle.

Maybe it wasn't a good idea to tell him all of this. But if he can't deal with it, then I'd rather know now. It'll kill me if he decides to leave me.

We finish our picnic, then sit quietly and watch the sun set. It's intense—the reds and oranges make it look like the sky's on fire.

"Are you okay?" I finally ask him. He hasn't said a word for the last ten minutes, and I'm starting to get worried.

"I know you're wondering if this changes the way I feel about you. Well, it doesn't. I love you. But it's a scary situation, the mafia is no joke."

"I love you too. But if you can't do 'us' anymore because of who my family is, I understand." He grabs me and we fall back on the blanket.

"I'm not going anywhere, Gia. Stop trying to give me an out."

I'm so fucking relieved. It may take him a little time to get used to things. But he loves me and I think we'll be okay.

Chapter Fourteen

Giovanna

This will be the first holiday season we will spend with our family. And it's the first for Declan and me. The Laurent boys will be joining us right after Christmas and staying through the New Year.

Our town takes the holidays very seriously. The entire town is decorated in lights and my papà said it's been this way since my grandfather came here from Italy.

The entire family is here. My papà has even allowed Declan to stay at the house with us. In his own room of course, but that doesn't stop us from snuggling in my room for hours till he sneaks back to his. It's like we're teenagers.

Declan

Being here with Gia is everything I thought it would be and more. I have to talk to her dad about my Christmas gift to her. I want him to know how serious I am about her.

I'm also still trying to get my head around the fact that her dad is the fucking head of the Chicago mafia. Holy fuck. I'm in love with the daughter of a man that could end my career, my life, with one phone call. She claims they're 'legit' now, but I've heard the stories about the old days and the feud between the Italians and the French. Add in knowing that Gia and Enzo were kidnapped by the head of the French Mafia—it's terrifying. Now I understand why Gia has Grady, and Rella has Marco—even their mothers have guards.

I see Enea coming out of his super-secret office. I call it his 'Bat Cave' because the door is built into the wall and you can't see it if you don't know exactly where to look.

"Enea, do you have a minute? I would like to talk to you, please." I can hear my voice shaking as I talk to him.

"I do. Why don't we go into my office," he says.

I follow him back into his Bat Cave. It's a really cool office. There are no windows. Instead, pictures of the family cover the walls. I smile as I see a few of Gia. I stop and look at a picture of their family where the kids were all tiny. This must have been before Gia and Enzo were kidnapped. She was such a beautiful baby and I can't help imagining our own little girl. I find myself smiling, thinking of my future with Gia.

"What is it you wanted to talk to me about?" Enea asks.

I sit down in front of his desk and clear my throat.

"I want to ask you for permission to marry Giovanna," I blurt out. "I don't mean right now, I want to plan my proposal. But I want to ask you now so that you know how much your daughter means to me."

Enea is staring at me as I vomit out my speech.

"It really hasn't been that long that you and Gia have been dating." He frowns.

"I know. But I also know that she's my whole world. I go to bed thinking of her, I get up thinking about her. I can't wait to get home when we have away games so that I can be near her."

He's still staring at me and I'm starting to sweat. I don't even get this nervous before a game...

"You understand that if you hurt my Gia, there will be consequences. You will never get a second chance to be with her."

My eyes probably resemble saucers as I nod at him.

"I would never hurt her and I would never let anyone else hurt her either."

It seems like he's finally starting to relax.

"I will give you my blessing to marry Gia."

I let a huge breath out and wipe the sweat on my forehead.

"Thank you, Enea. You won't regret this."

He stands up and comes around to his desk. I stand up and he embraces me.

"Welcome to the family, Declan."

"Thank you." I'm still shaking a little as I follow him back out.

Giovanna

I yawn and roll over to look at the time. It's six in the morning, and it's CHRISTMAS DAY! We had a huge dinner last night with the entire family and today we're opening gifts, of course. After getting dressed, I knock on Declan's door and hug him when he opens it.

"Merry Christmas, my penguin," he whispers in my ear, holding me tight.

"Merry Christmas, amore."

We can hear my parents talking in the living room as we walk down the stairs. My brothers come barreling down the stairs like a herd of elephants, taking Declan and me with them. Weirdos.

"Okay, so tradition in the Mancini family is one person hands out the gifts, one at a time. This year the honor goes to Grady because he's had the hardest job of keeping mi passerotta Gia in line this past year."

I stick my tongue out at my papà as everyone is laughing. Grady is acting all dramatic about coming up to the tree to take his spot to hand out gifts. This family is crazy. But I wouldn't change any of it.

Declan

After all the gifts have been handed out and opened, I pull a little box out of my pocket and face Gia. I'm so nervous. No, I'm not going to ask Gia to marry me today, but I am giving her something I hope she'll love.

"My penguin, you are everything to me. It took me a while to figure out what to get you for Christmas. I mean, what do you get for the girl who can buy everything she wants for herself?" She chuckles softly listening to me. "So I chose this. You once told me it was one of your favorite things."

I hand her the little box and I watch as she opens it.

Giovanna

I gasp a little when Declan hands me the box. I open it and find a shiny platinum ring. It's a claddagh ring, which has so much meaning. *Love. Friendship. Wealth.*

Declan pulls the ring out of the box and shows me the inscription inside of it. "*My penguin. Sempre*".

I watch him as he puts it on the index finger of my right hand. Then I hug him tight.

"I love it so much. Thank you, amore."

I look over at my parents and they're smiling. For once my papà isn't trying to kill Declan with his eyes. It's a Christmas miracle.

I turn back to Declan and I pull out a box similar to his. It dawns on me that our gifts are similar. I had a pendant custom made for him, it's a claddagh, and the back is engraved with the words. "*Sempre. My penguin*". I take it and fasten the chain around his neck, then watch has he picks it up to look at it. A smile spreads across his face.

"Thank you, baby. This is the best gift anyone's ever given me."

I kiss him and then hug him.

Best. Christmas. Ever.

Declan

Today's game was a shit show. We never really got it together and kept making stupid mistakes. We ended up losing 7-6. I was in the box three times tonight. I've never been in the box three times in one game. It's my fault we lost—it was my last penalty that they scored the winning goal on.

I haven't seen Gia in over three weeks now and I've barely been able to talk to her. We're both so tired that we end up falling asleep while we video chat. She's shadowing a few of the doctors at Cambridge Memorial Hospital back in Boston. It's not routine shadowing—she's an excellent student and because of how well she did at Crimson, they called her to see if she wanted this opportunity. It's only for a month and this is her last week. So she's been really busy. I was supposed to see her last week, but she canceled at the last minute because she had to study. I almost got on a flight to see her since I had two days off.

I'm so pissed about tonight's game. I need her and she's not fucking here. The only good thing right now is that I'll see her tomorrow. But tonight? I plan to get drunk with Dom and Cillian, then go and pass out. I already tried to call her, but she's at the hospital tonight and can't talk until her break. Fuck me.

"I miss Gia so much. Three weeks is too fucking long. I won't go this long again," I grumble to Dom.

"I know, man. But you'll see her tomorrow." In the months that I have been with Gia, Dom has been one of our biggest supporters. I'm not sure if Bastian and Enzo are as thrilled, but at least Dom understands.

Cillian stumbles back to our table and orders another round.

"Fuck, I miss Rella," he grunts.

"Tonight was so fucking bad. I can't believe I let that asshole provoke me into fighting." I slam my drink and take another from the waitress.

"Fuck it. It's over now and we have a week off," Dom says.

We watch as a group of girls sashay over to us as we drink our beers.

"You boys look lonely," one of them says, running her hand down Cillian's arm.

"Please don't touch me." He glares at her.

"Aww come on, baby. We can show all three of you

a good time," another says while she tries to sit on my lap.

I immediately stand up and she falls on her ass. "Sorry. But don't sit on me, I'm not a chair."

All I want is for them to go away and let us drink in peace. Or if Gia could walk through the door to be with me, that would be even better. Although I'm afraid that if I talk to her right now, I won't be nice. Not because I'm mad at her, I'm just so frustrated about this damn game tonight.

"I can come back to your room and you can help me feel better," the girl says to me. I put my hand up so she can't get any closer.

"Not going to happen. You and your friends need to leave." Dom and Cillian are telling the other two girls the same thing.

"Come on. We all know how you hockey boys are," I hear one of them say.

"I don't know what you've heard, but I don't do one-night stands and I would never cheat." These are the kind of women that worry my Gia. I know she trusts me, and I would never break that trust. No one is worth losing my girl over. No one.

She laughs."I know your ex is pregnant with your baby. That means you're going to be a daddy and you cheated. How does your 'girlfriend' feel about that?" She actually used her hands for the air quotes. What. The. Fuck.

"That's none of your business. You shouldn't believe everything you read. Or hear." I go back to my beer and ignore her. She tries to lay her hand on my thigh, but I stand up again. I wave at the bouncer who comes over.

"Everything okay, Mr. O'Reilly?" he asks as I shake my head no.

"Could you escort these ladies out? They're disrupting our night."

He herds all three of them away.

"You probably can't get it up anyway!" one of them yells at me, making me snort. Fuck, I miss Gia. I pull out my phone to see if she's texted back yet. Nothing.

"They seem to get worse every year," Dom says.

"They're getting worse!" Cillian barks out. I snicker at him. He's swaying as he says it. Maybe it's time to go back to the hotel. If I can sleep, then tomorrow will be here sooner.

Giovanna

For the last few weeks, I've had the opportunity to shadow some of the doctors at Cambridge Memorial. It's not an opportunity that you could say no to. But it's meant that I've had less time to talk to Declan and I had to cancel my last trip to see him. I know he was disappointed. I wanted to ask him to come to me, but I knew I wouldn't have any time to spend with him. This is my last day of shadowing. It's been an eye-opening experience, I know now that I definitely want to go into surgery.

I head to the break room and finally get to sit down. This shift has been nonstop. First thing I do is call Declan but it goes straight to voicemail. I check how the game went tonight and see the Redhawks lost. It was really bad. Declan was in the box three times during the game. I've never seen him in the box that much. I try Dom next and it goes straight to voicemail too, so I text Rella.

Giovanna: Have you talked to Cillian tonight? I missed a call from Declan but now he's not answering and neither is Dom

Fiorella: No. I missed Cillian's call cause I was in the shower. I tried to call him back, but he didn't answer AND he hasn't called me back

Giovanna: WTF. Why aren't they answering? Declan never ignores my calls…

Fiorella: Maybe they don't have service where they are? Remember the other away game? They didn't have service there

Giovanna: Ugh. I'm off in two hours. Let me know if you hear from Cillian. Love you

I put my phone down so I can grab my turkey and

roast beef sub. I love when my mam visits. I get homemade sandwiches instead of instant ramen.

> Fiorella: I will. You let me know if you
> hear from Declan or Dom. Love you too

I browse the internet while eating my sub. I'm excited that Declan will be here tomorrow. But I still wish I could've been there with him tonight. It kills me to know that he's going through this alone.

> Giovanna: Hi baby, I'm sorry I missed
> your call earlier. Tonight's been so
> crazy. I saw what happened. I'm sorry
> about the game. I tried calling you…
> I'm off in about two hours. Please call
> me back. I love you.

Declan

I feel my phone buzz and I pull it out of my pocket. I have a missed call from Gia. "Fuck. Why didn't my phone ring?" I mutter to myself as Dom looks at me. "I missed Gia's call." I tap her name to call her back, but it goes straight to voicemail. I start to leave her a message, but her text comes through so I hang up. Dammit. Now I feel even worse. I order more shots for the three of us. At least those girls are gone.

Declan: Amore…We seem to be
playing phone tag. We're at the bar
just having a few then heading back to
the hotel to sleep. Hope you're having
a good night. I miss you so fucking
much. I'll try you again later or you call
me when you get off. I love you

I slam shots as I sit and mope. More girls come by and try to get us to buy them drinks. On a normal night, we at least chat with fans but tonight all I want is my Gia. It's fucking crazy how much I want her around all the time.

We drink for another hour and then stumble back to our rooms. Cillian and I are rooming together, Dom is sharing the room next door with another teammate.

I fall asleep thinking of Gia. I can't wait to see her tomorrow.

Giovanna

After my shift is over, I look at my phone and see that Declan tried to call. I miss him so much. I try to call him, but it goes to voicemail again. So I text him instead.

Giovanna: Hi, my love, I'm headed
back to the house and to bed. I hope
you're okay. Call me if you get this.
Otherwise I'll see you tomorrow. I can't
wait. I miss you so fucking much too

I make my way over to where Grady is waiting to drive me home and get in the car.

"How was your shift?"

"It was good. Super busy. But good. Have you heard from Dom? Or maybe Declan or Cillian?"

"No. I saw the game, though. It was brutal."

"I read about it. I missed Declan's calls, and now he's not answering his phone. I tried Dom, but he's not picking up either."

"They probably went to have a few drinks."

"Yeah, that's what he said in his text. Phone tag sucks. I just want to hear his voice. Especially after a game like this."

"I know, sweet girl. But I'm sure they're okay. They'll be here soon."

"I just miss him a lot."

He parks at the dock and we get out, then head to the boat. "This is the longest we've gone without seeing each other."

"I know, but you're almost done here and then you'll be back home."

"Feels like a lifetime," I grumble.

"You'll find your rhythm eventually. This is the first time you're trying to balance his career and yours." He puts his arm around my shoulders as we dock at the house.

I take a quick shower and check to see if Declan called or texted. I sigh when I don't see any new notifications. Fuck. I try calling him again and it goes straight to voicemail. I frown at my phone like it's going to explain to me what's going on. I huff at it, then switch to looking online.

I tap on an article about tonight's game. I see a picture of Declan in the box. He looks so angry. I feel even worse that I wasn't there to support him. I make a promise to myself that I'll be there for the next game no matter what. My finger slips on the page and another article opens up. The headline reads: *Chicago Redhawks Lose to Pittsburgh*, and underneath that it says, *Star Players Find Solace In Local Fans*. There's a pic of a woman draped on Cillian and another on Dom. It's the third picture that makes my stomach turn. It's Declan with a woman sitting on his lap. She looks like she's whispering something in his ear.

I feel like I'm going to be sick. I know that reporters like to hype things that aren't real. But after not talking to him all night, and his phone still going straight to voicemail...

Chapter Sixteen

Giovanna

Sebastiano and Grady have been staying with me here in Boston for the last few weeks. Because it's my last week, Rella, Sal and Luca decided to come visit. Enzo arrived yesterday—he said he missed the island, and we don't know when we'll be coming back. I love having them all here, it makes the time go by faster. Not only that, the Hawks have the next week off, so Declan, Dom, and Cillian are supposed to be here soon. But after all that shit last night, I don't know what's going on anymore.

"Hey, Giovanna!" I hear one of my former classmates, Krista, calling for me. "A bunch of us are going to sing karaoke tonight, you and your sister need to come with us! And no saying no. You always say 'no'." She giggles as she takes my arm and drags me with her down the hall. "Plus I know you're leaving soon and we need to hang out before you do."

I keep telling Krista that Fiorella is my cousin, but she insists on calling her my sister. It makes me laugh every time. "Okay, okay, what time and where?"

"Seriously? YAY!" She claps. "Moonlight Lounge on O'Donnell Street at 7 p.m. We can eat there too, it's gonna be so much fun!"

"I'll have to bring my brother and some other friends too."

"Don't you flake or I'll come to your house and drag you out," she teases. "Is that your brother?" She stares at Bastian.

"Yup. This is Sebastiano," I introduce them. "Sebastiano, this is Krista."

"Nice to meet you. Ready, Gia?" He looks at me.

"Ready."

"7 p.m., Gia!" Krista calls out. She's still staring at Bastian.

"What's at 7 p.m.?" he asks.

"We're all invited to dinner and karaoke." The look on his face makes me laugh as we get in the car.

"Hell. No."

"Come on. It's one night."

"What do you think Declan will say?"

"I don't know, and right now I don't care. We played phone tag all night. He was supposed to be on the jet this morning, but as far as I know, they never got on it. And I haven't heard from him at all today. So I don't really give a fuck what he thinks." I take a deep breath. "I haven't been able to get a hold of Dom either. He's probably off being stupid with Declan and Cillian."

"Fuck. I'm sorry Gia. But maybe it's not what you think? I mean Declan isn't an idiot. He would never give you up for a piece of ass. And Dom probably let his phone die. You know how he is."

"Who's side are you on, Bastian?" I snap. We get out at the dock and get on the boat.

"Don't even ask that, Gia. You're my sister. I'm always on your side."

"Then stop trying to make excuses for him. We're all going out tonight and we're going to have a good time. I have the next seven days off and I was going to spend it with Declan. But he's not here and I don't know where he is." I pull out my phone and show him the pictures that I saved from that article. Then, I get off the boat and head inside. I tell Rella the plan for dinner and karaoke, then I head to my room to take a nap.

Sebastiano

I could kill Declan O'Reilly, Cillian McGregor, and my twin. I call Declan and get his voicemail.

"Declan, it's Bastian. You bastard, you

better call me back right now or I'll call my papà and let him handle this. If he gets involved, you'll never see Gia again. I saw the pictures."

I hang up and text him the same thing. Then I call Dom.

"Dom you shithead where the fuck are you and why aren't you answering? Where are Declan and Cillian? CALL ME."

I text him my message.

Declan

I wake up with the worst hangover I've had in a long time. I look over and see Cillian on the other bed... then I look at the time.

"FUCK! CILLIAN!"

He moans for me to shut up. "We missed the fucking flight." I jump up and grab my phone. Seeing that it's dead, I plug it in as Cillian falls out of his bed.

Someone is banging on our door. I fling it open and Dom comes barging in holding his head.

My phone finally turns on and messages are coming in. Sebastiano's message is at the top.

FUCK.

I call him back.

"Declan you asshole, where the fuck are you guys? And what the fuck is with those pictures?"

He's screaming when he answers.

"Bastian, I'm sorry. My phone fucking died last night, I passed out without charging it. What the fuck is going on? Is Gia okay? Wait, what pictures?"

Cillian is throwing his shit in his suitcase and Dom is packing mine as I grab some clothes to go take a shower.

"Where is Cillian? Is he still with you? And Dom? Gia saw pictures online. Of the three of you with women."

"They're right here. We'll call the pilot now and have him get the jet ready. We'll be there ASAP. I don't know what pictures you're talking about."

I'm starting to panic and I feel like I'm going to be sick as I talk to Bastian. What pictures? I didn't touch any women last night. Then I remember those three girls who wouldn't leave us alone. FUCK.

"I don't know if Gia or Rella wants to see either of you. Let me find the pics."

That's exactly what I didn't want to hear.

"Please Bastian, I need to talk to Gia. Is she okay?"

"Why didn't you call her right after the game like you always do?"

I tell Bastian how Gia and I played phone tag all night. I was actually relieved that I didn't talk to Gia. I was so angry about the game. It felt like the referees were making shit calls and then there's the three fucking penalties that I took. We lost the fucking game because of me. Pittsburgh scored the game winning goal on the third penalty. I didn't want to take it out on her. That turned into being angry because my heart and soul is in Boston. I want her with me. This is the first time I've had such a shitty game since I met Gia. I explain all that to Bastian. There's no point in lying about it.

I hear him sigh.

"I get what you mean, man. But Gia doesn't

think like that. She's already having a hard time with the women. You can't do this to her. And you should probably know she's getting ready to go out with some people from work. Rella's going too. Some bar with karaoke."

"We'll be on the jet in two hours. We land at 8pm."

"Okay, brother. I'll make sure someone is there to pick you guys up. You should try and call Gia."

Sebastiano hangs up.

I push past Cillian to grab a quick shower.

"Hurry up. I need to shower too so we can get going," Cillian grumbles through the bathroom door.

"Have you called Rella?" I ask him as I get out of the bathroom.

"I tried, she isn't answering and won't respond to my texts."

Cillian shoves past me to get in the shower.

"Fuck. Gia isn't answering mine either." Dom frowns at his phone like that will make her answer him.

I call Gia. It goes straight to voicemail which means she's either turned her phone off or she's set it like that on purpose. Fuck. I leave her a voicemail.

"Amore mio, please call me. Bastian told me about the pictures, it's not what it looks like, just some drunk fans. Please baby. I'm so fucking sorry. I need to talk to you. I love you so much."

I send a text too.

> Declan: Gia, I just tried to call you. My phone died after I came back to our room. That's it, nothing happened. Please call me back, baby.

Giovanna

I hear a text come in with Declan's tone. I turn towards my phone as I finish getting dressed. Hearing a knock at my door, I open it. Enzo and Bastian walk in. Bastian looks at my phone and sees the texts from Declan.

"Are you going to answer him?"

"Why should I?" I finish getting ready. Bastian finally looks at what I am wearing.

"Oh hell no. You aren't going out like that."

I'm wearing jeans, heels and a halter top.

"You're my brother, Bastian. Not my papà or my husband. So yes, I'm wearing this tonight. Who's coming with Rella and me?" I ask as I look at him.

"Everyone's going. Marco will leave later to pick up the dumbasses. You need to change."

I ignore him about changing.

"What dumbasses?" Rella asks as she joins us in my room. "Are we ready to go?" Her phone makes Cillian noises. She silences it.

"Dom, Declan, and Cillian are getting on the jet. Someone has to pick them up."

"What? Why? Just leave them there." Rella shrugs.

"Do you really want me to do that? Cause your papà and mine will find out what's been going on. Right now, it's just us. But if they get involved, they will make you leave Cillian and you, Gia? You'll never see Declan again."

Sal and Luca come in while Bastian is talking.

"You know Bastian is right. If Papà finds out about last night, he won't be happy about it."

Rella rolls her eyes at Luca. "Then don't open your big mouth."

"Right now I don't care. Let's just go and have some fun," I add in.

We all head downstairs and out to the boat.

"Marco, you head to the airport in two hours," Bastian says to him.

"So, bring them back to the house? Or to the bar?" Marco asks as we're getting off the boat.

"Bring them back here. We don't need them causing a scene at the bar," Sal says as the guys nod in agreement.

When we get to the bar, I see my classmates and introduce everyone.

"You all know Rella. These are her brothers Salvatore and Gianluca, my brothers Sebastiano and Lorenzo, and that's Grady and Marco." Then my classmates, "This is Adam, Mattias, David, Krista, and Simone."

"So did all of you have the same classes as Gia?"

"Yeah, we were all in the same classes when she was at Crimson. But since she abandoned us, it's like we're missing a limb." Adam chuckles.

"I wish you were still with us. And you never told us why you had to leave." Krista pouts.

I hug her. "I know. It's a long story. I promise I'll tell you one day."

Declan

"You get ahold of Rella yet?" I ask Cillian while we walk to the jet.

"No. She still won't answer me. I think she turned off her phone." He rubs his face and looks down at his hands. "I can't lose her."

We board the jet and get settled. I look out the window and shake my head at myself. How could I have been so fucking stupid? I did the exact thing that would hurt my Gia the most. Those damn pictures.

Reporters are vultures that will make a story out of nothing.

"I know, man. I know." He looks like he's going to throw up…I hope he doesn't do it here.

Giovanna

We finish eating just as the karaoke portion of the evening starts. We're relaxing, watching the people going up to sing when I hear my name being called by the DJ. I know I didn't put my name in. I look at Rella, who's giggling.

"You suck, Rella." I laugh. I make my way up to the stage and I hear the music start for Aretha Franklin's Natural Woman. I hear cheering and I know it's my family. I blush as I start to sing.

"Holy shit, she's good," Mattias says to Rella.

"She is. She's been singing for a long time."

Krista orders a round of drinks and shots for the table.

"Just a Coke for me. I'm the 'DD'," Grady explains when Krista asks him what he wants to drink. She nods at him and puts the order in.

I finish the song and everyone's clapping for me as I sit down. We take the shots as we toast to our group being back together.

"Sing a song with me," I hear Mattias ask me.

"Sure." I smile. "What song?"

"Do you know *A Whole New World?*"

"I do know that one." I answer as he goes over to the DJ to put the song in for us.

"Okay, he said there's like four people ahead of us." He tells me.

"Gives me time to drink more."

"Watch it, Gia," Enzo murmurs beside me.

"Don't tell me to watch it." I whisper angrily to him. Lorenzo sighs at me.

Everyone cheers after each singer. Before I know it, it's our turn to sing.

Sebastiano

I start a group text with Dom, Bastian, Sal, Luca, Declan and Cillian.

> Sebastiano: So what the fuck? You three are the biggest assholes. Someone better fucking explain those pictures

> Cillian: We did nothing wrong. We lost then drank. Then came back to the hotel and fucking passed out. What pictures? Send them. We don't know what the fuck you're talking about

I shake my head. I send all three pictures and the article so they can see the headline.

Lorenzo: How long till you land?

Gia and Mattias go up to sing.

Declan: Fuck. That's bullshit. Those
fucking women wouldn't leave us
alone. That picture of me was right
before I dumped her on her ass and
told her not to fucking sit on me

Domenico: He's not lying. Those girls
were fucking crazy. And none of us
touched them. Those pics are bullshit

One thing I know is that my twin doesn't lie to me. Even if it could save his ass.

Declan: We're landing now. Where are
you guys? I need to see Gia

Lorenzo: I'm not telling you where we
are so that you can come here and
make a fucking scene

Cillian: Come on, Enzo. Rella won't
answer my calls. I need to talk to her

I watch my baby sister up there.

That Mattias guy is getting way too close to her while they sing. I fume as I drink my beer.

Chapter Seventeen

Declan

We get off the jet and see Marco waiting for us in the car.

"How was the flight?"

"Bumpy," Cillian grunts.

"Take us to Gia and Rella please," I say, tossing my suitcase into the car.

"I can't, man. My orders are to take you to the house only." He actually looks a little sad as he says this to us.

"Come on, Marco," Dom says. "Gia won't even answer my calls."

"Please. I have to see Gia." I can see the conflict in his eyes, then he slowly nods okay.

"The guys are going to kick my ass for this."

"Thanks," we all say, settling in for the short drive.

Giovanna

Mattias and I finish the song and walk off the stage. He stops and kisses my cheek. I put my hand on his chest to push him back.

"I can't. We can be friends but I can't offer you anything more than that."

"Why not? Are you with someone?"

"Yes, I'm with someone. I came out tonight to have fun. Let's just sing, drink and have fun okay?"

The DJ comes over to let us know he's picked a few songs for us. People in the bar are requesting for us to sing together.

Declan

The first thing I hear when we walk into the bar is my Gia singing. God I missed her voice. When I hear a guy's voice, I look up at the stage. He is standing way too close to my baby while they sing together. I start to head that way when Grady stops me.

"Don't do it," he says in my ear. I stop to look around and I finally see the rest of the group at a table.

Cillian sees Rella sitting close to some guy. He stalks over as Marco starts to go after him.

"What the fuck are you three doing here?" Sebastiano snaps.

"We have to see if they can work this out. I don't know what it's like to be in love. But I do know I would like my boys to back me up if it was me," Marco says to Bastian while he's trying to stop Cillian from making a scene.

I can see the turmoil in Bastian. He finally agrees with Marco and relaxes.

"Fine. I'll try to help you with Gia."

"Thank you, brother. I promise I would never hurt her. She's my life. And I swear, those pictures? They don't show what really happened." I look at my soul up on stage singing with a guy I don't know. He needs to take his fucking hands off of her. I want to go up there and grab her to show him that she's mine. In fact, that's exactly what I'm going to do.

"I'll talk to Gia and Rella too," Dom says. I nod and thank him.

Giovanna

I see Declan stomping towards the stage looking like an angry bear. I look over at Mattias and his eyes get really big. Declan is a big guy—six foot five, and about two hundred and seventy pounds. When he gets mad, he looks even bigger. Mattias is about six foot even and maybe one hundred and ninety pounds. Unfortunately he's not moving away from me because he has no idea that I'm with Declan.

"Isn't that Declan O'Reilly? Do you know him? He plays for the Chicago Redhawks." I hear him as our song ends and we return the mics to the DJ.

"There are more requests for you," he says. "I'll give you two a break for like, thirty minutes."

We thank him, then make our way off the stage. I try to walk past Declan.

"Baby, stop. Please." He touches my arm.

"Did he just call you 'baby'?" Mattias turns to look at me, his eyes look like they're going to pop out of his head.

Well, fuck. "I'll meet you back at the table."

"Are you sure you'll be okay? He looks really mad. I don't want to leave you with him."

"I'll be fine."

Mattias leans in to kiss my cheek, but I step back from him.

"You. Need. To. Walk. The fuck. Away. NOW," Declan growls loudly.

"I'll be okay." I push Mattias towards our group. I glance at the table and see Rella going off to the side with Cillian.

"What do you want, Declan?"

"Why was he standing so close to you? Why was he touching you? And why did he try to kiss you?" he snaps.

"You had your fun last night and I'm having mine now," I snap back at him as he pulls me to the side.

"You're mine, Gia. No one touches you. I did nothing last night except get drunk and pass out. I didn't touch anyone and no one touched me. Those pictures you saw? That was taken right before I dumped her on her ass. I told her not to sit on me. Please, baby. Dom will tell you the same thing."

"Fuck you, Declan. You don't get to ignore me all night, miss your fucking flight and then come in here acting like a fucking caveman trying to stake your claim. And that girl? That was just the icing on the cake." I finally see an emotion from him besides anger.

"Nothing happened. We drank too much and passed out. My phone died so I didn't have an alarm," he says, stepping closer to me.

"Whatever. You'll never stop being who you are, Declan."

"And who am I, Giovanna?" he snaps angrily.

"You're a player. You like having women throw themselves at you. You like them screaming your name at the games. Well I won't be the little wife just sitting at home, waiting for you to come back whenever you feel like it. I won't be your second choice." I try to turn away to walk back to the table.

"Dammit, Giovanna! You're not fucking second. You will never be second. There's no one I want except you. Forever. You can't just walk away. I won't let you. This is us—you and me. I would never, and I mean never do anything to hurt you."

We hear the DJ call Mattias and me to come up and sing again as the people in the bar cheer.

"Ready to sing some more?" The whole group is approaching, and Krista grabs my arm, oblivious to the anger radiating off of Declan.

"Oh god. What are you guys planning?" I giggle. They pull me away from Declan. Adam is pulling Rella with him.

The music for "Summer Nights" from the movie Grease starts up. I can't stop laughing. We're singing it just like in the movie. If you've seen it, you know this song and how it plays out. We're at the part where they sing about making out and holding hands. Mattias kisses my hand while smiling at me. I look over at Declan, I can see that he's fuming. I can also see the muscles in his arms and chest flexing as he watches Mattias. Then, there's the part in the song where they ask if he could get him a friend. Adam grabs Rella and kisses her cheek. She's laughing while he's holding her.

Sebastiano

Out of the corner of my eye, I see Cillian jump up and leap towards the stage. I jump up to stop him, along with Marco.

"Don't do it, Cillian," I say low enough for just him to hear. I see Declan moving towards the stage and Grady grabbing him.

"Can we let you both go now?" I ask as Grady continues to hold Declan back. They both nod as we see the group heading off the stage and towards the tables. Cillian makes a growling noise at Adam and he jumps away from him. I nod at Grady to let Declan go and we watch as he heads straight for Gia.

Giovanna

Declan grabs me and takes me to a darker area of the bar.

"Why are you doing this?" he says quietly. But I can feel him shaking.

"Doing what, Declan? Showing you how it feels to see the one person you love most in the world with someone else? I didn't plan this, I didn't ask him to touch me. In fact, I told him we can only be friends. That I'm with someone."

He kisses me roughly and as passionately as he can.

I bite his lip hard enough to draw blood, but he just growls and pulls at my jeans to get them down. He turns me around and I hear his zipper going down, then he pushes into me.

"Declan, fuck!" I gasp.

"You're mine, Gia. No one can or will touch you. Ever." He grunts while he starts to move faster, his breath getting ragged.

I moan and grip his hands as he moves faster. My orgasm hits me right as he's coming.

"Fuck!" He grinds himself as far into me as he can. He holds me tight as he shoots his cum into me. I lean my forehead on the wall. My heart is beating so damn fast.

I slowly turn to face him. "This doesn't change anything. You can't do what you did last night and pretend it's okay," I say, pulling my jeans up.

He's always come to me after a bad game. It hurt so much last night when he didn't. And then there's those fucking pictures.

"I wasn't with anyone but Dom and Cillian last night. There hasn't been anyone else since the day I met you. I got drunk, then passed out in my room alone last night—well, Cillian was there. You're my heart, my soul, my life. You know that I would never, ever cheat on you. But yes, I'm an asshole because instead of talking to you after the loss last night, I chose to drown myself in alcohol. I felt sorry for myself. I wanted you with me, I handled it all wrong. I'm so fucking sorry, amore."

"Is everything okay?" Enzo asks, coming around the corner.

"We're okay, Enzo. I think it's time to go home." I head back to the group to let them know we're leaving.

"Aww. But promise you'll come out again sometime," Krista says, hugging me, then Rella.

"I promise. Maybe you can come visit us in Chicago."

Mattias comes up to me last. "Are you okay?"

"I'm okay. Thank you for singing with me tonight."

I step back and take Declan's hand.

When we get back to the house, Cillian tries to follow Rella into her room, but we hear her slam the door in his face and lock it. Then we hear him begging her to let him in.

Grady and Marco do a sweep of the house, heading outside to check the perimeter. They make sure all the doors and windows are locked, then check the security tapes to make sure everything is running properly.

Declan follows me upstairs into my room and wraps his arms around me.

"Don't, Declan."

"Why? You're mine, Gia." My phone dings. He sees a text from Mattias as he hands it to me.

"Do you like him?"

"Sure. He's a nice guy."

> Mattias: Hey beautiful. I just wanted to check and make sure you're okay. I was worried when you left. I wanted to tell you I had a really great time tonight and I hope we get to hang out again

"That's not what I meant and you know it."

"No, Declan. I don't want Mattias. There's only one man in this world that I want. And he's standing in front of me." I can see him relax as he looks at me. I love him so much it hurts. "I'm going for a swim." Swimming has always helped me to relax.

"Can I join you?"

I hesitate for a second then nod at him. He gets changed and we head to our pool.

Declan grabs towels along the way, and throws them onto the lounge chairs. We have a rooftop pool, I open the glass roof so I can see the night sky. I dive into the pool and hear Declan dive in after me. He swims up to me and nuzzles my neck.

"I swear to you, Gia, I didn't do anything. I just let my anger win and I drank too much. I would never do anything that would hurt you or us. No matter how drunk I get. I can't live without you."

He turns me in the water to face him. He kisses me slowly and gently. I kiss him back, wrapping my legs around his waist. I nibble the spot right below his ear and hear a soft rumbling sound coming from him. He nips the sensitive spot right over my collarbone. I rub myself on him and I feel his cock getting harder.

"Show me what I mean to you," I whisper as he gets

his trunks off. He pulls my suit to the side and slides into me.

"Fuck, my love. It's only you and me. Forever." He slowly pumps in and out of me as I hold onto him tight. I close my eyes as he starts to move faster.

"Forever, amore," I gasp, climaxing around him. I hear him groan as he releases in me.

"You only get this one chance, Declan. Never again."

"I won't need another chance. I'll never shut you out again, ever, I promise you." We float around and talk until I start yawning.

We get out of the pool. I dry off and wrap the towel around me as I look at another text from Mattias.

> Mattias: You have the most beautiful voice and I can't wait to sing with you again. Get some rest. Sweet dreams (heart emoji)

> Giovanna: Thank you. Good night

I put my phone on my night stand then head into the shower. Declan comes in behind me and we rinse off together. When we're done, we lay down on the bed and Declan turns on the TV.

I grab my phone to text Rella.

> Giovanna: Hey Rella, give Cillian a chance to make it right. I believe Declan about those pictures being bullshit. He said the one of him and the girl? It was right before he dumped her on the ground. And Dom backed his story

I see the little dots on the screen and wait for her response to come through.

> Fiorella: SIGH. You're sure? Dom's not just protecting him?

I read it and then look at Declan who is starting to doze off. God, he's beautiful.

> Giovanna: Yes

> Fiorella: Okay. He won't get another chance though

> Giovanna: That's what I told Declan. This is the one and only chance he gets. Love you

> Fiorella: Love you too

I hear Declan's breathing even out as he falls asleep. I take the remote, put a movie on, then lie back and snuggle into him. His arms hold me tight even when he's sleeping. This is home for me.

Chapter Eighteen

Giovanna

After what happened with Declan last month, I came to realize that I need to confront Dorian if I wanted to get past some of my insecurities. Lorenzo and I have been talking and we decided it's time. I'm hoping this will help both of us to heal. I don't know if I can ever truly forgive him and I mourn the loss of all the memories we should've had with our real family.

The hardest part about this whole thing is that we had a wonderful childhood. We never felt like we didn't belong or that we were unloved. But that doesn't make the lies any easier to deal with. In fact, it makes it harder, if we had a shitty life, I could just hate Dorian.

Looking at Enzo, I take a deep breath and squeeze his hand. Then I call Chris.

"Hey sis, how are you doing?"

"I'm doing okay. Are all of you free today?"

"I'm sure we can all find time. What's wrong?"

"Nothing's wrong. Well not really. Enzo and I were talking and we think it's time to talk to Dorian. To find out once and for all why he took us."

"Okay. Where do you want to meet? I'll bring Pa—I mean Dorian."

"Merci, Chris. Let's meet at the Grand Hotel in Naperville. I'll book the suite now and we'll see you in three hours?

"D'accord petite sœur. See you soon."

"See you soon."

I hang up while Enzo goes to tell Grady and I head to our papà's office. I knock, then open the door after I hear him say to come in.

"Hi, Papà. So we're meeting Dorian and the boys in three hours at the Grand Hotel in Naperville."

He stops what he's doing and looks up at me from his seat at the desk. "Are you sure you're ready for this, mi passerotta?"

"Sì, Papà. I need to do this and I know Enzo does too. It's time."

He draws a deep breath, stands and comes over to me. He holds me and kisses my head.

"You make sure Grady's with you at all times. Maybe you should take Arturo?"

I look up at my papà. "Dorian won't hurt us, Papà. Grady will be fine. We don't need Arturo." I can see the worry on his face.

I hug him tight, then kiss his cheek. "Okay, Papà, we'll take Arturo too." The relief in his eyes is noticeable as he calls Arturo in and tells him he'll be coming with us.

"I love you, Papà."

"I love you too, mi passerotta."

Lorenzo

I sit and listen to Gia talk to Chris. I'm glad she's finally ready to talk to Dorian. I think this will be good for both of us. I need to stop being angry all the time. I know for a fact I'll never forgive Dorian for taking us. But I can be at peace with it, I hope. I tell Bastian and Dom about our plans.

We let Grady and Arturo know that we'll be leaving soon. They already know the plan for today. Our papà isn't very happy about it, but he knows that we need to do this.

I see Gia come out of our papà's office with him following behind her. I go over and hug him.

"Be smart and be safe," he says to us and we nod.

"We will, Papà," I say as we leave with Grady and Arturo.

"Wait! Why can't Bastian and I come with you? The Laurent boys are going to be there, right?" Dom says as he stares at Gia and then back to me.

"Can you promise not to interfere?" Gia asks softly. We watch the expressions on our older brothers' faces.

They turn and look at each other and then back to us, both saying yes.

"Okay," she says, and our papà looks even more relaxed knowing that we're all going together.

Giovanna is quiet the entire two hours it takes for us to get to the hotel. We leave the car with the valet, and head into the lobby where we see our brothers waiting. Arturo goes to check us in and get the key cards while Grady stays with us.

We hug Chris, Fabien, François and Jérôme. Dorian steps forward to hug Gia, but she steps back and stands next to Dom. I can see the hurt in Dorian's eyes, but I won't hug him either.

When Arturo comes back, we all head up to the penthouse suite. We spread out on the couches and just stare at each other.

Dorian sits with his sons but I can see his eyes are glued to Gia. Every once in a while he looks at me. I can see how hard this is for him too. But it's his own fault.

Giovanna

"Why?" is all I can get out. I watch Dorian stare down at his hands as he thinks about his answer. "And don't lie to me. I can't take anymore lies from you. I want the truth."

"*Princesse*...You have to understand—" he starts to say, but I interrupt him.

"I'm not your princess. You don't get to call me that anymore." I can feel my anger rising.

"I'm sorry. I wish there was a better reason besides it was the 'old days'. War days. I never intended to hurt either of you."

"But you took us. You claimed that we were left alone and you found us. Was that a lie?"

"It was. All four of you were in a room together. You were all sleeping. I knew I couldn't take all four of you and looking at the three boys, I could tell you two were identical." He looks at Dom and Bastian. "I knew about the double set of Mancini twins. So I made the decision to take you and Lorenzo." He sniffles as he talks.

"So I didn't imagine you." We all whip our heads

around to look at Domenico. "I saw you walking out. But I didn't know you took them until my papà and mamma came in to check on us. My mamma screamed when she couldn't find Enzo and Gia," he says, his voice cracking. "She spent the next year silent. She didn't speak to anyone. Not even Sebastiano or me. You did that to her."

My tears fall freely as I hear the pain in Dom's voice.

"You bastard," Sebastiano says softly, glaring at Dorian.

"I can't say I'm sorry enough times. Back then, all I wanted to do was bring your father down and secure my place in my family. Our fathers were the ones that were really at war. And I knew I had to prove to mine that I was worthy of running our clan." He doesn't look at any of us as he says this.

"Why didn't you return us?" I ask. "Why did you keep us? Why did Nadia go along with this?"

"By the time the war was ending, your mamma... Nadia was gone. And I was so angry about losing her. I know I should've taken you back. I knew that if Enea found out I was the one who took you, he would have to do something to show that they had the power. I couldn't take that chance."

"So you just kept us? Didn't you think that one day we might find out what you did?"

"I didn't let myself think about it. You were both happy weren't you? I love you both the same as I love

Christophe, Fabien, François and Jérôme. Never any less."

Lorenzo

"That's not the point! But is that what you want to hear? YES. We grew up feeling loved and wanted. But the bottom line is, you stole us from the ones who should've loved and raised us. You took that away from us and them!" I yell at him and he seems to shrink in his seat. "You're only sorry because it's all come out! If Bastian and Dom hadn't seen us that day, we would still be living as Laurents."

I hear Gia sobbing next to me. I hold her and growl at Dorian when he reaches out to her.

"Don't touch her. You had no right to keep us. I understand the war, but you could've done the right thing anytime in the twenty-three years you had us. Maybe then I would've been able to forgive you."

"I know there's nothing I can do or say that will change the past. All I can say is that no matter what, I love you both." He turns to Sebastiano and Domenico. "I'm sorry I hurt you boys and your parents. When I think about it now, I don't know what I would've done if someone had taken any of my boys. Your father showed maturity and strength by not coming after me. And I know it was because he didn't have the proof he needed to do it, but most men would have retaliated without it. Not Enea Mancini, and that's why he has the empire that he does now."

His tears are falling as he finally looks up at both of us.

Giovanna

I stand up and look over at Dorian.

"Thank you for telling us why you did it, but I can't be here anymore, knowing that you took us from our home with my brothers sleeping right there. And that they had to endure my mamma not speaking to them for a year? That's more than I can take right now. I don't hate you, that takes too much energy. Maybe one day we can sit and talk again, but for now—I need to leave."

I turn and walk towards the door with my brothers, Grady and Arturo following me. I stop, remembering that Christophe, Fabien, François and Jérôme are here. I go over and hug them as tight as I can. *"Toujours mes frères,"* I whisper to all of them. *Always my brothers.*

"Toujours," they say to me. *Always.* I walk back out while Dom and Bastian wait for Enzo.

I hear Dorian sobbing. My heart is breaking for him despite what he's done. Maybe now he'll understand what my parents went through when he took us, the pain and sadness they had to endure for the twenty-three years that we were gone.

I feel stronger having talked to him. Even though I understand the life of a mafia family, and the pressure to be the top boss, this is still not something I can just forgive. But maybe in time I will.

Chapter Nineteen

Declan

Hockey season is almost over and if we win tonight, we will be headed to the playoffs for the first time in five years. The last couple of years we came close, but this year has been outstanding. I know my Gia has brought me good luck. I watch the boys go through their pre-game rituals and I smile to myself. Athletes are such superstitious people. When something brings us luck? We stick with it till it doesn't. I kiss the pendant that Gia gave me for Christmas, then make sure it's sitting under my pads so that it can't get ripped off if I get into a fight.

"This is our year, boys! Win or lose tonight you're all champions and I'm proud of every one of you," Coach Rossi says to all of us.

Everyone cheers and chant, "Hawks!"

Holy fuck, we won. WE. WON. We're headed to the first round of the Stanley Cup Playoffs! I see Gia jumping around and hugging Rella as they cheer with the crowd. She makes me feel like I'm Superman.

The playoff format is three rounds of up to seven games each. To advance each round, you have to win four out of seven games.

We are tied 3-3 in round one, and tonight will determine whether we go on to round two or if our playoff time is over for this season.

For tonight's game, like every game since the playoffs have started, I have my good luck charm with me. Things with Gia are a lot better now. After that disastrous weekend, we made sure we saw each other as much as possible. It wasn't always easy to do, but we both needed it.

During the playoffs, Gia and Rella have been traveling to every game with us. This weekend we're in New York. Having Gia in the stands, knowing that she's here for me, gives me the boost I need.

We get on the ice to do our warmups. As I skate by where Gia is sitting, I tap the glass with my stick as I pat my heart. I see her smile as she mimics what I just did. God, she's beautiful.

Giovanna

I copy Declan when he skates over and pats his heart. That man has made me stronger. I've put him through so much and he's never stopped fighting for me.

I can't wait to see the team win the cup. They haven't won it in ten years. I think this is their year. I smile as Cillian blows a kiss to Rella as he skates by.

"You two are so lucky," we hear someone say behind us.

I turn around and smile.

"Thank you," Rella and I say together.

We watch the guys head off the ice after they warm up.

I stretch. "Let's go and get some food. We have twenty minutes."

"What do you want to eat? Maybe a hot dog? Or a burger?"

"Hot dog. I feel like when we're at games we need to eat hot dogs."

She chuckles. "And fries. Don't forget the fries."

Marco and Grady are looking around. Crowds make them crazy because they're unpredictable.

"I'm so nervous. I want them to win tonight, but if they do, we'll have to do this again for the second round. I don't know if I can handle it."

"I know. But they can do this, they deserve to win." I'm doing my best to sound confident. Inside I'm nervous as hell, but I'm trying to hide it. I'm so proud of Declan and the team.

"Last year was so hard for Cillian when they lost the game they needed to get into the finals."

"I know, Rella. But this is their year. I can feel it." We get our food and go back to sit in our seats. Our seats are right behind the Redhawks bench again. It's the perfect place to be able to see our guys as they get on and off the ice.

This game was so close! At one point they were tied, and we thought we'd be going into overtime. Then in the last minute of the third period, Declan scored the winning goal.

The Redhawks won 3-2! We are up on our feet and cheering as the New York fans are booing and starting to leave. Rella and I are jumping around, cheering and hugging each other.

"Round two, here we come!" I yell as we watch the

guys skating around the ice, celebrating. Declan, Dom and Cillian all smack the glass with their sticks as they skate by us.

Round two was just as nerve wracking as round one, maybe more. Our boys did it in four games. The fourth was won in triple overtime, which means it lasted an extra two hours. You could see the guys were tired. Cillian made the final goal that sent us to the semifinals.

Next, they need to win the semifinals. It never gets any easier to watch them play. Whenever Declan gets hit, I cringe. Then I want to get onto the ice and beat the shit out of the asshole who hit him. Yeah okay, I know it's part of the game, but he's my baby. I don't like it.

It feels like the momentum from the wins they're getting is helping them. They're playing faster and more aggressively as the series goes on. The team will have two weeks off because they won this round in the shortest amount of time possible. It's a good thing though, because they need the rest. Declan and I are headed back to Chicago for a mini vacation.

The semifinals played out just like the first round. It went all the way to the seventh game. It was so fucking intense. The teams were tied and we went into double overtime. There was so much adrenaline in the building, you could feel it in the air. It was Milo who shot the winning goal, and the building erupted. It's a great time to be a Chicago Redhawks fan.

"We're going to the finals!" I scream as Rella and I jump up and down.

Because it's an away game, we can't go to the locker area to wait for them. So we'll meet them at the hotel and celebrate there. We're in the car with Marco and Grady heading back to the hotel.

I decide not to change out of my jersey as we wait for the guys to text us and let us know they're here.

I hear my phone chime with Declan's tone and I smile.

Declan: We're on our way to the hotel. Meet us in the bar?

Giovanna: How long till you get here?

Declan: Maybe 20 min. Be ready to party!! I love you!

Giovanna: I love you, baby!

I laugh as I show Rella his texts. She's laughing at my texts and at Cillian's as we wait for them. About ten minutes later we head down to the bar to wait for the team and hear a commotion.

"I think they're here."

The guys stop to take pictures and sign autographs for fans.

We all cheer as we see the team getting closer. I see Declan and run over to him, he picks me up and kisses me.

"Congratulations, baby!" I laugh as he spins me around.

"Thank you, amore! I'm so glad you're here with me. Next round is in two weeks."

"This is your year, baby. I just know it!"

Rella and I head to the bathroom and run into Josie.

"What the fuck is she doing here?" I whisper to Rella.

Josie is now about eight months along. The last time we figured she was lying, but this time we can see she's not. I just wish she would stop coming after Declan. She's still claiming it's his baby. So as soon as the baby's born, we'll do a paternity test. I already know it's not his, but our lawyer says we need to do it this way or it'll never end.

Josie follows us into the restroom.

"You know that when our baby is born, Declan will

be a big part of his life, right? And yes, it's a boy. He'll finally have a son to teach hockey to—our baby will be just like his daddy."

I just stare at her.

It takes a lot not to just tell her to fuck off. The most frustrating part is the wait to get the paternity test done so she can be gone from our lives once and for all. I use the bathroom, and when I come out of the stall, Josie is still there. I ignore her as I wash my hands and see Rella come out of another stall. She's glaring at Josie as she washes her hands.

"Are you ready for Declan to leave you when our son is born?" She smirks at me.

"Why don't you just find the real father and leave us alone?" I'm trying to keep my anger in check.

"Declan is my son's father. And in a few months, you'll see the truth too. I know he told you we hadn't been together for a while, but he's lying. We've never stopped seeing each other. Away games are the best."

I take a deep breath and walk past her. Because it would be a bad thing for me to hit a pregnant woman, right? Take the high road, Gia, take the high road, I tell myself as I hear Rella snort at Josie. I love my cousin.

I make my way over to Declan and give him a hug.

"Josie's here," I whisper to him, then see him frown.

"What the fuck? Why? What happened?"

"Same shit. She's saying it's your baby. Apparently she's having a boy. And that when he is born, the test will prove he's yours. Then you'll leave me so you two can be together. Oh and that you've been seeing her this whole time and she's with you for away games. I just wish this was over." I lay my head on his chest.

"I know, amore. It'll be over soon. Tonight is for celebrating. Forget about her. You're my good luck charm."

"Thank you for not giving up on me." I truly don't know where I'd be if he had.

"I told you at the beginning—you're mine, Gia. I meant it then and I'll mean it fifty years from now. You're the best thing that's ever happened to me. I just wish my parents could've met you."

"You know, Declan, you really should be coming with me to my appointments to see our son," Josie's voice hits us.

"Just stop, Josie. We all know I'm not the father of your baby. I'm sorry you can't move on, but I have." He takes my hand and we walk over to where Dom, Rella and Cillian are.

"She's crazy." Dom laughs.

I sigh. "I just hope once her son is born and the test is done, she'll finally move on,"

"Fuck it. Tonight is for celebrating! We're in the FUCKING STANLEY CUP FINALS!" Cillian yells causing the entire team to cheer and start chanting, "Redhawks!"

Chapter Twenty

Declan

I don't think I've ever been this nervous about a game before. Tonight is the last game of the playoffs. Tonight, one team will be Stanley Cup Champions. Winning the cup is something I dreamed about as a kid, but win or lose, I have so much to be thankful for. I have the best girl, the best team, and the best family. I send a silent prayer to my parents, something I do before every game. It's because of them that I'm here. My parents loved hockey. They always drove me to practice and came to every game.

I start my pregame ritual and observe all the guys in the locker room. You can feel the tension in the room. It's not an uncomfortable tension, more like an excited hum in the air.

"We got this. No matter the outcome tonight, we're still winners," Coach Rossi says. "We've come so far this year, and for that you should all be proud of yourselves. I know I am."

We head out to the ice for warmups. We're playing our final game at home, and winning here tonight in front of our home fans would be a dream come true. The Redhawks have never won a cup on home ice. We need to fix that right now.

I see my girl and skate over to her. I tap the glass with my stick, then pat my heart. I see her smile and pat her heart as she mouths, I love you. I mouth back, always. I feel like I'm floating as I return to warmups.

Giovanna

The atmosphere in the arena is crazy. Our home fans are super excited, and it's only getting louder as the guys come out for their warmups. Declan comes over and we do our ritual of him tapping the glass and then patting his heart. I smile and pat my heart as I mouth, I love you. I see him mouth back, always. That man is my heart.

Tonight's the night—everything is coming together for him. I can't seem to stay still as I watch him warm up. I've never been so nervous and excited at the same time.

The whole team has smiles on their faces while

they warm up. I've never seen Dom so happy. I look around the arena and see people holding signs for the team.

"You want to get some snacks before the game starts?" Sal asks everyone.

Technically we can order from our seats and they'll deliver it to us. But it's nice to go and walk around sometimes, too. Especially tonight.

While we walk around, people stop to high five us and say good luck. Redhawks fans are awesome.

Declan

We won. Holy shit, we won. We are the Stanley Cup Champions! The best part was being able to win at home. The crowd is on their feet! The fans are cheering so loudly it feels like the arena is shaking.

We all gather to wait for the trophy presentation. First they will award the trophies to the players. The team not only won the Stanley Cup, we won the Clarence S. Campbell Bowl.

The crowd goes wild as Domenico wins the Vezina Trophy, and Cillian wins the Hart Memorial and Art Ross Trophies. I won the Conn Smythe and the James Norris Trophies. It's been an unbelievable night and it's not over yet—I still have something planned. I'm so damn nervous. Even more nervous than when we first got on the ice tonight.

The crowd is still on their feet chanting, "Hawks!" We all take turns skating around the rink with the cup. After I pass it off to Cillian, I go and find Gia who is making her way down to the ice with the whole family. Her Laurent brothers are here tonight, too. I go to her dad first—he hugs me and slips me something that I've been holding onto for a while now. I go over to Gia, pick her up and hug her tight.

"You did it, baby! I'm so proud of you!"

I put her down slowly and drop to one knee. I look into her glittering green eyes. The crowd seems to quiet down a little. It feels like a bubble has surrounded Gia and me.

"Giovanna Aoife Mancini, tonight has been one of the best nights of my life. Winning the Stanley Cup has been a dream of mine from the first day I stepped onto the ice. Help me make it even better—say you'll be my wife. My partner. My penguin. My everything," I say as my team surrounds us. "Will you marry me?"

Giovanna

I'm staring at Declan. He's down on one knee asking me to marry him right here in front of everyone. I can't believe he's doing this. I feel myself nodding and finally get it out.

"Yes!"

He slips the ring on my finger and stands up to twirl me around.

I lean in and whisper. "Tonight will be a night you will never forget. Not only did you win the Cup and your trophies..." I pull out tiny knitted ice skates and hand them to him.

"Gia?" He's looking at the tiny skates and I can see he's trying to figure out what it means. All of a sudden he breaks out into a huge smile. "SERIOUSLY?" His eyes are glassy with tears, I nod at him as my tears keep falling. "Baby! I love you so damn much."

We head back over to my family, and they all hug us one by one. The team is surrounding us and everyone is celebrating. The crowd is back to chanting, "Hawks!" It's a sound I know I'll never forget.

Epilogue

<u>Four months later</u>

Giovanna

It's been a year and a half since my life changed. So much has happened since the day I found out that Enzo and I had been kidnapped. Some good and some bad, but I wouldn't change any of it.

I lost a papa, but gained a family. I found Declan. Through all of this, he's been the best thing ever. He said he would never give up and he never did. He stuck with me through all my crap. We had a few bumps along the way, but we've found a way to make it work, together.

These last three months have been so crazy. After the Redhawks won the Stanley Cup, Declan, Dom and

Cillian were signed for a record eleven year contract with the Redhawks. So we'll be staying in Chicago for a long time.

We also had the paternity test done for Josie's baby —Declan's not the father, of course. She was so angry that she demanded they do the test a second time. The results were the same. She finally admitted the father is the same guy she had the one night stand with. The same one that ended her relationship with Declan.

It's been so much better with that chapter finally closed for us, hopefully for good.

Declan and I got married a month ago today. We chose to have a small ceremony in the same church that Declan's parents were married in. It was just our families and his teammates. Declan said he wanted to make me his wife before the baby came and I'm due in two months. We have chosen not to find out the sex of our baby. Except now that it's getting closer, I think I do want to know. But I'm trying to hold strong and wait.

Declan

I'm not sure anything can top this past year. My team accomplished something every hockey player dreams of—we won the Stanley cup. I was also lucky enough to win two of the defenseman trophies. But what I've found in my personal life means even more to me. When I lost my parents, I dreamed of finding a love like theirs one day.

When I met Gia, I had almost given up on finding my soulmate. That's what my parents called each other. I truly believe that if my dad hadn't passed away the night of the accident, my mom wouldn't have given up. I've never been angry about it, because even back then, I understood their love for each other. They didn't love me less, they just couldn't live without the other.

Now that I have Gia, I understand that better. I don't know if I could go on without her.

We got married a month ago and now we're waiting to meet our baby. We have names picked out for a boy and a girl. If it's a boy, Rowan Enea for our fathers, and Savannah Gráinne for our mothers.

Bonus Epilogue

<u>Two months later</u>

Giovanna

I had our son a week ago. We named him Rowan Enea O'Reilly. He's the most beautiful baby I've ever seen in my life. Right now he has his daddy's eyes and I hope they stay this shade of green. He got his dimples from the both of us and his curly auburn hair from me.

I look over at Declan, who's holding Rowan and talking to him as Rowan stares up at him. I know exactly how he feels when he looks at his daddy. I look at him like that every day. I'm in awe of the man that he is. I couldn't ask for a better husband or father.

Declan comes to sit on the couch with me. "Thank you for giving me everything I've ever wanted," he says.

He kisses me. We hear Rowan squeak between us and we chuckle.

"Thank you, amore. You've done more for me than I could ever ask for. You helped me out of the darkness that I thought would swallow me whole."

"Just one more request." He gives me that mischievous look.

"What's that?" I look into his beautiful green eyes. I would say yes to anything he asks of me.

"I'm going to need more babies. Lots more." He kisses me, then gives me that beautiful smile that I love.

About the Author

Hi! I'm Natalie. I published my first book, Aftermath in August 2021. I've been lucky enough to find my own insta-love-at-first-sight person. We have a daughter who drives us crazy and a corgi who adds to the chaos. I love hockey (Chicago Blackhawks), MotoGP (Motorcycle Racing), and baseball (Chicago Cubs). When I'm not writing, you can find me studying or crafting. Or crafting when I should be studying.

Nataliearthurbooks.com

Sebastiano

I had given up on meeting my person, content to be the protector of my family. Then one day I met her. But someone else was laying claim to her. If she was happy, I would step back and watch her from afar. But then I saw the marks on her and I knew I needed to save her.

<u>Schuyler</u>

It seems like I've been struggling most of my life. Just my sister and me against the world. Then I thought I met the man of my dreams. Turns out he's the man from my nightmares. I can't run and I can't escape from him. Then I met Sebastiano. He made me feel safe from the moment he took my hand in his. He says I will be his, but he doesn't know about the monster that's in my life. The one that won't let go.

Saving Her is the second book in my Mancini Legacy Series. All books are standalone, but it's best if read in order. There is mention of characters from my Cimaruta MC Chicago Series.

https://books2read.com/SavingHer-ManciniLegacy

Luciana

Women on an MC council? It's unheard of until now. Love at first sight? That's a new one for me too. I was convinced I didn't need someone to make me happy.

Then I slammed into Rónán.

Literally.

In an instant, he turned my world upside down. But can he handle the MC life?

<u>**Rónán**</u>

My life was going the way I planned it. Then the most beautiful woman stepped into my path and changed my life forever. I know she's keeping things from me. And that's okay...for now.

Because she's mine.

She just doesn't know it yet.

Choices is the first book in my Cimaruta MC Chicago Series. All books are standalone, but it's best if read in order. There is mention of characters from my Mancini Legacy Series.

https://books2read.com/Choices-CimarutaMCChicago

Francesco

I met the love of my life at fourteen. She had my heart the moment I saw her. But when you're young and stupid you don't always make the right decisions. That's what happened to me. I let the temptations of my job distract me from the one thing I couldn't live without. I had lost all hope, but fate gave me another chance. I have to make it up to her. I know she's hiding something from me. Will she let me in and give me a second chance?

<u>**Maeve**</u>

I thought I had it all. Sure I may have been young, but when it's real, you just know. That was, until he ended things. I never saw it coming. Now he's back and he wants another chance. Can I really trust him not to break my heart again? I want to believe him. I've never stopped loving him. But it's not just me I have to protect anymore.

Can they find their way back to the happily ever after they were meant to have? Or will they be pulled apart again, shattering all hope?

Reclaiming Our Forever is the second book in my Cimaruta MC Chicago Series. All books are standalone, but it's best if read in order. There is mention of characters from my Mancini Legacy Series.

https://books2read.com/ReclaimingOurForever-CimarutaMCChicago

<u>Amante</u>

Relationship? No.

Love? Hell no.

Forever? Never.

A quick hook up and that was that. I had my family and my club and that's all I needed. Until the day she walked in. With her I wanted more than one night, but when I got out of

the shower she was gone. But I will find her. Then I'll just
have to convince her we belong together.

<u>Charmaine</u>

Love is nothing but a lie. I watched my parents crash and
burn and nothing and no one could change my mind. Until
him. My tattooed, hunky biker man. Wait, did I say mine?
That can't happen. But he says all the right things, and makes
me feel like I'm the most special girl in the world. Can we
make it work?

**Notch the Plan is part of the Notchin' Boots
Series. There is mention of characters from my
Mancini Legacy Series and my Cimaruta MC
Chicago Series.**

https://books2read.com/NotchThePlan-NotchinBoots

<u>Hollis</u>

The people you're born to don't always turn out to be your 'family'. Families can be chosen, and I chose the Cimaruta MC. They've been there with me for the last six years, and I thought I had everything I needed. One night was all it took to make me want more. But she's hiding something from me and I need to know what it is. I will save her from anything. That much I do know.

<u>Lila</u>

My life was finally going smoothly. It was me and my daughter against the world. I worked at a club called Club Curve—I'm a curvy girl, so why not? Then one night, HE walked in. Now he's turning my life upside down and I'm not sure how to feel about it. My biggest fear is about to become a reality.

Just as you are is a stand alone and part of the Club Curve series. But there is mention of characters from my Mancini Legacy and Cimaruta MC Chicago series.

https://books2read.com/JustAsYouAre-ClubCurve

Kostas

Mating matches keep the peace in our world. So why did it feel like my life was over when it was my turn? She hated me from the moment we were paired. And to be honest? I hated her too. So when she rejected me for some loser from another clan, it didn't bother me that much. But then I met her—the one the fates chose for me—and everything just felt right. I knew in an instant that she was the one I would never let go of.

Artemis

In our world, mates can be either fated or chosen, but finding your fated mate is never guaranteed. I thought I had chosen someone who could love me and we would spend our lives together. But then he rejected me—for my BEST FRIEND. That day, I decided I was fine being alone. But then, completely by chance, I met someone who felt like home. Could this really be it? The forever I secretly craved...my fated one.

My Fated One is part of the Fated Mates Series. There is mention of characters from my Mancini Legacy Series and my Cimaruta MC Chicago Series.

https://books2read.com/MyFatedOne-FatedMates

<u>Aiden</u>

Motorcycle racing has been my life since I could walk and talk. It was all I ever needed. Or so I thought. Then I met the one woman that made me want more. One day, the unthinkable happens—a racing accident causes me to lose all my memories of her. But I still feel her in my soul, even if my brain can't remember her.

<u>Élodie</u>

I wanted a knight in shining armor, but what I got was a wolf in disguise. After escaping from him, I met a man willing to give me everything I ever wanted. Then in a split second, he was taken from me. Not physically, but mentally. The man I love doesn't remember who I am, but I'm determined to get him back.

Racing Back to Love is part of the Forget-Me-Not Series. There is mention of characters from my Mancini Legacy Series.

https://books2read.com/RacingBackToLove-ForgetMeNot

9 781963 504002